All Fall Down

Grandma Kookum,
Hope this one keeps you
up late reading!
I love you ~
Julie

Other books by Julie Coulter Bellon

Through Love's Trials

On the Edge

Time Will Tell

Be Prepared: A Parent's Guide to the Eagle Scout Award

All's Fair

Dangerous Connections

Ribbon of Darkness

All Fall Down

A Novel by

Julie Coulter Bellon

Cover Design by LibrisPro
Copyright 2012

ISBN -13: 978-1479264858
ISBN-10: 1479264857

Printed in the United States of America
First Printing September 2012
10 9 8 7 6 5 4 3 2 1

For my sweet Brinley—you were worth the wait. I love you!

Acknowledgments

I am so grateful to the people who love and support me in my writing. I could never do this without you.

Thanks to Jan Holman, Debra Erfert, Jodi Bezzant, and Robyn Wood who patiently read this story in different stages (sometimes multiple times!) and kindly pointed out where it could be improved.

Jon Spell heroically read the manuscript in sections with several stops and starts and offered some great advice (and dialogue ideas, too!)

Curt Lowe (and Robyn Wood) offered me guidance and knowledge on guns and law enforcement that was invaluable.

Gary Daynes and Pat Holman have been valiant home teachers and graciously accepted their "punishment" for missing a month or two. I hope you both smile when you read this.

Jordan McCollum and Emily Clawson have saved my writing sanity with their incredible critiques and I am in awe of their never-ending patience with my manuscript. Thanks you guys for all the laughing and late nights. You're amazing.

And last, but never least, my greatest thank you goes to my husband and my children who are the center of my world. I love you more than words could ever say.

Chapter One

Something was wrong. Rafe could feel it. He'd opened the door to the building that housed his family's business, but hesitated before going in. The hairs on the back of his neck stood straight up. With a cursory glance into the lobby of the building, he couldn't see anything wrong. Chalking it up to being in Afghanistan too long, where he relied on his senses to stay alive, Rafe went in, tugging on his collar. Maybe that was it. He was reacting to the civilian uniform of a shirt and tie when he'd rather be in his Navy SEAL gear. *It's not like I could have shown up in desert cammies and boots,* he thought. But it might have been worth it to see the look on his brother's face if he'd walked into the meeting dressed like that. Vince was always a little obsessive about appearances.

Glancing up at the second floor landing where people could enjoy the atrium, Rafe swept the area for anything out of the ordinary and saw a man intently watching him. Stepping forward to get a closer look, the man noticed his interest and turned, disappearing. Rafe went to the elevators, all of his senses on alert now. *Should I go to the second floor? Am I over-reacting?*

With a grimace, he tried to loosen his tie, just a little. It felt harder to think when he was buttoned down with a tie, but as he quickly mulled it over he decided it was an over-reaction. Some guy watching him didn't mean anything was wrong. It could simply be his subconscious urging him not to go in because he'd been battling with himself all morning about coming. Ever since Vince had been made acting-president, he'd been making demands on everyone and Rafe planned to say no to anything Vince asked him. Their father would be on his feet soon and Rafe would be back in the field when his knee healed. There was no point in starting anything with Dad's business. Rafe wasn't planning on being here longer than he had to be. He pulled on his tie again, definitely regretting the choice of attire.

He took a deep breath and ran an impatient hand through his longer-than-normal hair. The air was humid, and from the looks of the pewter gray sky on his way in, Rafe knew they'd have rain before the afternoon was out. *And rain will make my knee ache,* he thought with an inward groan.

Realizing how much his injury had taken over his thoughts, his actions—his life—he made a promise not to dwell on it any more today. Men wearing shirts and ties just like him strode through the lobby, getting to their jobs where they belonged. *Will that ever be me? Could I be happy working inside all day?* With how ugly the last mission in Afghanistan had been and how slow his knee was healing, he knew he might have to think about that in the near future. But not today.

He got into the elevator, the hairs on the back of his neck prickling again. *Stop it. Nothing is wrong.* He looked around the elevator, just to reassure himself. Two men in suits and a woman in the corner, watching him. Nothing dangerous. Rafe gave the woman a smile and turned back around. *Everything is fine. I'm going to meet my baby brother and get the 'you-could-help-me-around-here' routine. I'm going to say no. Then I'm going to visit Gary. There's nothing to worry about.*

The elevator dinged as they reached his floor and Rafe put a smile on his face. At least he could look forward to seeing his old friend Gary Holman. Gary had gone through SEAL training with Rafe from start to finish and they'd served together in Afghanistan. When Gary was wounded in combat and sent home, Rafe had recommended him to his father because of his computer skills. The rest was history. From what Rafe could see Gary was happier than he'd ever been. He couldn't wait to kick back and relax with him like old times.

Rafe got off the elevator and headed toward his dad's office. Axis, Inc., had grown a lot. It had started out as a corner office and small reception area, and had now expanded to fill the entire eighth floor. Computer forensics was a booming business these days, apparently. Rafe stopped mid-stride to look at the receptionist desk, trying to hide his surprise. Instead of the familiar receptionist his father had employed for years, there was a young woman with curly blonde hair down her back. She looked up at him with a large smile on her face, her long, obviously fake lashes nearly touching her eyebrows. Rafe couldn't turn away, but knew it was rude to stare. "Can I help you?" she finally asked.

"Uh, no." He watched her give him the once-over. Her lashes seemed to have a life of their own as she blinked rapidly. "I have an appointment." He walked toward the door that led to the offices, but found that it was locked. "New security?" he asked, turning back to the mini-me of Tammy Faye Baker who was now standing at her desk. *Why didn't I take my father's private elevator from the parking garage?*

"What was your name?" She smoothed her skirt down, calling attention to the length of material. Or lack thereof.

"I'm Rafe Kelly. I'm meeting my brother Vince."

"Ohh." She came around the desk, her impossibly wide smile even wider. "Are you the Navy SEAL? Vince told me about you. I'd be happy to swipe you through."

She wobbled a bit walking toward him and Rafe's eyes slid to her ankles. Her heels had to be at least six-inch platforms. It was a wonder she could walk at all. As she drew near, she wobbled again and he reached out an arm to steady her.

"Thank you." She stared up at him, her blue eyes as calculating as an accountant at tax time. "I'm so clumsy sometimes."

She pressed herself against his arm and Rafe politely stepped back. With a wink, or maybe a long eyelash blink, she grasped the card hanging from the lanyard around her neck. Leaning over to the door's security panel, she swiped it, practically posing for Rafe as she did so.

Rafe wanted to roll his eyes at her blatant attempt to flirt with him, but he maintained a polite smile. *Maybe if I don't react . . .*

Nope. "My name's Penny," she said, her voice a little more breathy as she straightened and took his arm again. "You know, I always show up, just like a shiny new penny."

Rafe raised his eyebrows. "Isn't the phrase a *bad* penny always turns up?"

"Well, if you put it that way," she practically purred, running her hand up his arm, stopping to squeeze his left bicep. "I'd be happy to turn up to show you my bad side. Or even turn up somewhere you're going to be."

Rafe kept his smile pasted on his face, but moved his arm back an inch to free it from her manicured grasp. He wasn't unused to female attention—being a SEAL got him his fair share, but he wasn't looking for it right now. And she definitely wasn't his type. Trying to imagine her hiking, or swimming, or doing anything he liked to do was nearly impossible. *High maintenance.*

He reached for the door handle that now had a flashing green light to the side of it, anxious to be out of this awkward situation. "Thanks, but . . . I don't think so."

She stepped toward him, cutting off his ability to escape unless he wanted to knock her off her high heels. "If you change your mind, you know where to find me."

Rafe resisted the urge to be rude. *Does she treat everyone this way? Is that why Vince hired her?* He made a mental note to at least ask Vince

4

what had happened to Genevieve. She was professional and had worked for Axis from the beginning. His father wouldn't have fired her.

He opened his mouth to say 'I have to go,' when the elevator behind them dinged, announcing an arrival. They both turned at the sound and Penny moved away from him to head back to her desk. "Thank you," Rafe said on a sigh of relief, glancing back to see who had saved him from that uncomfortable situation with Penny. The hairs on the back of his neck stood up again and with a start of surprise, he recognized the familiar figure that walked out of the elevator, looking around as if he were lost.

"Gary," Rafe called, turning toward his friend. "Are you just getting back from lunch?" He stretched out his hand. Gary's burns had faded a lot more in the last few months, the grafts making his injured face look so much better. Everything was looking up.

Rafe was about to pull him into a hug, but Gary reared back, his eyes darting to the people around them. He wiped sweat away from his brow, putting his other hand into the pocket of the very large jacket he was wearing. "Gary, what's wrong?"

At that second, Gary drew out a gun and when he did, his jacket parted. Strapped to his chest was what looked like the weapon prototype they'd been testing in Afghanistan just ten months before. "Rafe, I need you to come to the roof with me. Right now," he choked out.

Rafe held out his hands, hoping he was coming across as conciliatory. *Is this a PTSD episode?* "Gary, let's talk about this. Whatever this is about, I can help you."

Gary shook his head. "I don't have a choice." He waved toward the bomb. "You've got to come with me now or the bomb will detonate."

Turning back to Penny who seemed frozen at her desk, Rafe said sharply, "Call 911. Now."

He headed for the stairs with Gary. Looking at his friend's desperate face, Rafe sucked in a breath. It hadn't been an over-reaction after all. Something was definitely very wrong.

Chapter Two

"Ring around the rosy, a pocket full of posies," grated over the headset. The man's voice sounded shakier than the last time he'd recited the children's rhyme.

"He's reciting it again." Claire stabbed the mute button with her finger. "No matter what I say, that's all I get back. How am I supposed to negotiate for a hostage if all he'll do is repeat 'Ring Around the Rosy?'" She chewed on the inside of her cheek. "Do we have any psych reports on this guy?"

"Nothing new. We've got the president of the company coming in to give us some idea of what we're dealing with here." Captain Reed shuffled the papers in his hand—the same ones he'd read three times already. "I need a status report, people," he said into his radio. "Where are we?"

Claire heard their team check in. Almost done clearing the perimeter. Evacuation is ongoing. Stairwells are cleared and elevators locked down. But it didn't seem to satisfy the captain. "Where is this company president? I thought he was on his way!" He spoke to no one in particular as he paced, looking out the glass door as if the guy they were waiting for would magically appear.

Claire cracked her thumb knuckles. "You know I've got to go up on that roof."

"No way." Captain Reed's voice was firm. "Colby and Bart aren't in position yet. We need the information they can give us once they're in place." He brought the radio back up to his mouth. "We have a visual?"

"No, sir," Claire heard Colby's voice loud and clear on the radio.

"Captain, I can get us a visual. Let me on that roof. I won't be able to resolve this if I can't see him. I need to be there to read his body language instead of sitting down here listening to a nursery rhyme."

"It's too dangerous. You know that."

Claire looked over at her secondary negotiator, Steve Davis, for support, but he merely shrugged before glancing at the captain in front of them. The message was clear: he was the new guy and no way would he contradict the on-scene commander. Claire understood, but some situations needed more than one perspective.

With a small shake of her head, she pulled the mic of her headset down to her throat. Taking a step toward Captain Reed, she used her most reassuring tone. "I'll be fine." She drew herself up, giving him her most coaxing smile. It was a look she'd perfected for situations like this.

"Don't use your do-what-I-say-and-you'll-get-whatever-you-want tone on me," he admonished.

Claire pulled at the button on the sleeve of her blouse so she could roll it up. *It's always worth a try.* She turned back to the table and looked at her notebook buying herself some time to decide what to do.

"Just keep trying to talk to him. You know the drill—keep him calm and keep him talking. And a nursery rhyme is better than nothing. At least we know he's listening."

Claire released an inner sigh of disagreement and set her notebook back on the table. That was the problem, he wasn't *talking*

8

at all, and her listening skills alone wouldn't get a hostage out of there safely. She wanted to see this guy. Why was that so hard? She put the mic back to her mouth and took the headset off mute. "Gary? Can I call you Gary? Are you still there?"

"Ashes, ashes," he said through the phone, his voice hesitating a bit before he continued. "We all fall down."

"Are you sure there isn't anyone you'd like to talk to? I'd like to help you out of this." She licked her lips. All she could hear through the phone was the wind on the roof picking up and starting to whistle in the background. "Come on, Gary. It's not too late to go back. We can fix this."

There was silence on the other end for a moment and Claire shifted her weight from foot to foot, waiting. She wanted to push through the law enforcement personnel surrounding them and get up on that roof. It was only a hunch that she needed a face-to-face in order to end this peacefully, but it was a strong one and she'd learned long ago to go with her instincts.

"Ring around the rosy," he began again, his voice soft.

"Why don't you tell me what you want?" Claire rubbed her hand over her neck. A bead of sweat ran down her back between her shoulder blades. For the first time since this all started, Gary seemed to be fading a little. But what did that mean exactly? She would know if she could just see his face.

"Does that rhyme mean something to you? Tell me what it means and let me help you."

There was silence for a moment, then the heavy glass door behind her opened. A tall man in an impeccable dark suit and tie entered, staring at her expectantly. She cocked an eyebrow and muted her headset once again. He even had the little handkerchief in his breast pocket that matched his tie. "I'm Vince Kelly. Have you heard from my brother? Who's in charge here? What have you guys got?"

"Captain Ron Reed." He shook Vince's hand. "So far we don't have much."

Claire stuck out her hand and Vince shook it. "Detective Claire Michaels." *He's the president?* He looked like he'd barely graduated high school. She reached her hand back to grab her notes and double-check what they had on him.

"What more do you need? We've got to get my brother out of there." Vince unbuttoned his suit jacket and sat down. "The guy up there with him is Gary Holman, a fairly new employee."

"What do you know about him?" Claire asked.

"He has some pretty severe burns on his face from his tour of duty in Afghanistan. He served with my brother. I know he's good at his job here. Doesn't talk much. Keeps to himself."

"What did he do here exactly?"

"He works in our research and development department. He's got a lot of rough edges personally, but he has a great knack for figuring out encryption and finding hidden files."

"Is that what you do here?" Claire made another note, tapping her pen on the edge of the table.

"Yes, we write programs that help law enforcement with data recovery. You know, what criminals try to hide, we expose. We just got a big contract from the Department of Defense because of a program we developed for breaking encrypted files. What used to take months, we can do in days."

Either he really believes in his product or he's a slick salesman. Claire jotted down some notes in case she needed the information later.

"I hear you're the acting president of Axis. Where's the president?" the captain asked. The question came out a little too bluntly, putting Vince even more on edge.

"My father had a stroke. Listen, I could answer your questions a lot easier if I knew my brother was safe."

"We're just trying to get as much information as we can so we can get everyone out safely Mr. Kelly," Claire tapped her finger on her chin. "Has Gary been having any problems lately? Have you noticed anything unusual?"

Vince let out a breath and looked at the ceiling. "I don't know. I heard he might have had a few PTSD issues that he was dealing with. But he showed up for work and did his job. We weren't worried about it per se."

Claire straightened, going back to her position with the headset. "Do you think Gary would talk to you?"

Vince shrugged. "We could try."

She turned to the headset, taking it off mute, hope flaring in her chest for the first time today. "Gary, we've got Vince Kelly here. He'd like to talk to you." She handed him the extra headset.

Gary's voice came through as little more than a whisper as he recited the rhyme again. "Why is he repeating that?" Claire whispered to Vince. "Does that mean something?"

Vince closed his eyes for a moment and his face visibly paled. "Gary was a field expert in explosives. My brother told me that Gary used that rhyme when he was setting munitions, so they could make sure they all had time to clear the area. As soon as he said, *all fall down,* they took cover. It was an inside joke or something."

The hope that flickered in Claire's chest was instantly snuffed out. They had an explosives expert with PTSD on the roof with a hostage? Her mind reeled. *Think, Claire. Think it through.*

The room went silent as Vince began to speak. "Gary? It's Vince." He took a deep breath. "I don't know what's happening up there, but I don't think you want to hurt Rafe. You said once he's like your brother. Let him help you. Or I can help you. I'll do whatever you want, just let Rafe go." He was talking quickly, but he sounded sincere. Claire held her breath.

11

Vince's plea was met with silence. He said Gary's name a few more times, but Gary didn't say a word. With a defeated look, he handed the headset back to Claire.

Claire pushed the mute button, trying to quickly piece together a strategy. "Tell me again what you saw today, Mr. Kelly."

Vince folded his arms. "I was scheduled to meet with Rafe to talk over some family business, but was held up on an important phone call. When I was through with the call, Rafe still wasn't there so I walked out to the lobby to look for him. I could see through the glass doors that he was there with Gary. Gary pulled a gun on him. By the time I'd opened the security door, my brother was on his way to the stairs after telling my receptionist to call the police."

"Did Gary say anything to you?"

"No, I was too far away." He stopped and furrowed his brow. "I did notice he was wearing a tacky, plastic-looking jacket." His nose wrinkled. "And it looked like it had a matching black vest under it."

The captain shot a meaningful glance at Claire, but she pretended not to see. "What do you mean? What did it look like?"

Vince shrugged. "Like I said, I didn't get a good look at it. It just looked like he was trying to cover up a beer belly, which was odd since Gary is fairly fit." He smoothed his tie, obviously relieved he didn't have a belly to speak of. Claire doubted he owned any tacky jackets, either.

Now, more than ever, she needed to get up on that roof. She walked over to Steve. "Do we have any info from Bart or Colby yet?" She kept her voice low. Her two other team members should be in position by now and having eyes on the hostage-taker would tell her if there was a bomb up there or not. But Steve shook his head. "They're still trying to get a good angle."

She moved back toward her original position near the table, rolling her shoulders. "Can you tell us anything else about Gary's personality, Vince?" She turned back to the phone, ready to try again.

Vince shook his head. "I've already told you all I know. We need to get up there and get Rafe out."

Claire nodded her head. "We will, Mr. Kelly. I just have a few more questions."

Vince scrubbed his hands over his face. "Like what?"

"You said your brother was here for a meeting. Does he work here?"

"No, Rafe is a Navy SEAL, pretty highly decorated. He's only here on leave while he recovers from an injury."

Claire mulled that information over. "What kind of injury?"

"A knee injury." Vince shoved a hand through his hair. "Are we going to sit around and talk all day or do something? Maybe I should go up on the roof. Maybe if he saw me, Gary would give up or talk to me."

"I'm going up on that roof, Mr. Kelly, and I'll do everything I can for your brother, but first I need to make sure I have as much information as possible. Can you describe your brother for me?" Claire prodded.

"About 6'2" I guess," Vince said, finally sitting down in a chair.

"Eye color?"

"I have no idea. I don't stare into his eyes all that often. Green maybe? Blue?" He stood back up and started pacing. "Listen, shouldn't you be talking to him? What if Gary's done something to him already?" He reached for the phone headset Claire had left on the table. "I should try to talk to him again."

Claire noticed Vince was getting more agitated the more they talked, his pacing picking up speed. It was time to get him out of here, so she could concentrate on his brother.

The captain must have come to the same conclusion. He motioned for Vince to follow him to the door. "That won't be necessary. Detective Michaels has been trained for this situation.

We'd like to keep you close by in case we need you, so why don't you go down to our mobile unit and stay there. We'll keep you apprised of any developments." Vince looked like he was about to argue, but with a glance at the captain, he capitulated and was handed off to an officer right outside the door.

As soon as they were gone, the captain turned to her. "We're not taking any chances. Steve, get down there and make sure the entire building and surrounding blocks are evacuated." He stood over Claire, the commanding tone leaving no room for argument. "We're relocating to the mobile unit and if Colby gets a shot he's going to take the subject out."

"No. Not yet. That's always a last resort. You've got to let me go up there," Claire knew she had to try one more time. "We don't know for sure if that vest is a bomb, but if it is, I just trained on this. I can handle it."

"That was one seminar, Claire."

"One very *good* seminar." She gave him a half-smile. "Trust me."

He chewed on his bottom lip. "You're not going to let this go, are you?"

She shook her head. This was too important. Putting the mic to her mouth again, she spoke to Gary, but her eyes were on Captain Reed. "Gary, I want to come up and talk to you. Just talk. I'll be unarmed and I'm trusting you, okay?"

He didn't respond, so Claire kept talking. "I'm here for you, Gary. Anything you need. You just have to be willing to talk to me."

There was silence once again before she heard the familiar rhyme start up, his voice stronger this time. "Ring around the rosy, a pocketful of posies, ashes, ashes, we all fall down."

"Okay, I get that you don't want to talk right now. Is Mr. Kelly all right? Can I talk to him?"

Claire could hear some scuffling and she clenched her teeth in frustration. He was definitely a unique case by virtue of the repeated nursery rhyme alone. What was he trying to tell her? To take cover? Did he really have a bomb vest up there? Something else was going on here and she needed to look this guy in the eyes, see how close he was to the edge. She'd never wanted to see someone as badly as she wanted to see Gary.

"Claire, I want this taken care of as much as you do," her captain said, his tone softening.

Claire merely nodded, her entire focus on Gary. She could hear his breathing, shallow and fast and she knew the adrenaline was rushing through him, just like it was running through her system. "Gary? Is everything okay?" She shot a quick prayer heavenward. *Please, God, let him listen a little longer.*

After a long pause, Gary finally started to whisper the rhyme again and Claire swallowed hard, grateful to hear it. As long as he was reciting that rhyme, he was still alive and they had time to get the hostage out safely.

The captain grabbed the rumpled papers and read off their laundry list of information for the millionth time, his normally calm demeanor cracking a bit. "We need more."

His voice was low and tightly controlled, but Claire could hear the frustration.

"If it's PTSD, we have a chance to talk him down," Claire said. "He was probably seeing a counselor so we need to figure out who that was so we can get them on the phone." She paused. "I can go up and get him talking while you're gathering more information. We'll keep the team in position with him in their sights. I'll be fine." Claire folded her arms over her chest and stared directly at the captain.

The captain wasn't a man that let many people question his orders, but Claire had been part of his hostage negotiation team for so long, he cut her a little slack. He'd always trusted her instincts before and she'd proven herself on the job. She knew what she was doing, but for some reason the captain was in protective mode today. They all knew situations like this could get out of control in the space of a heartbeat, but in this instance she had a gut feeling and not being able to follow it was making her crazy.

Captain Reed ran his hand over the short gray stubble on his head, his military-style haircut the same today as it had been the day she'd met him six years ago. He obviously didn't want to give in and let her go out, but he was warring with the fact that he wanted this thing taken care of as soon as possible. "Okay, but I want you to stay on a safe perimeter, especially if there's an explosive involved. Don't get too close—this guy's on the edge. Literally."

Claire nodded, a small smile lifting her mouth at her captain's gallows humor. She quickly took her headset off mute before she spoke. "I'm coming out right now, Gary. And since you've been out there for a while, I thought I'd bring you a drink of water," she told him. "Do you think you can come away from the edge? It'd sure be nice to have a cold drink where it's not so breezy."

She didn't receive an answer.

She set the headset on the table behind her, watching curiously as Captain Reed looked over a piece of paper Steve had just handed him. "Do we have any water bottles?"

He nodded his head and wordlessly handed her the paper. The message said her father had called. Twice. *What's that about?* Claire pressed her lips together in a tight grimace. Her dad was the chief of the National Clandestine Service, which didn't give him a lot of time to actually be a dad. What would make him call now? Was it something to do with this case?

Captain Reed walked over to the corner of the room while she read, picking up a Kevlar vest for her. Handing it over, he watched as she crumpled the note. "I don't like this, Claire. Something doesn't feel right."

"Yeah, NCS could add another layer to this thing. I mean, involvement by any part of the CIA gives me a headache. You know how those guys are." Claire shook her head. Maybe her father was just worried about her. But he would know she was working. As soon as Vince had said Rafe Kelly was a highly decorated SEAL, it had crossed her mind that he could be part of any number of elite groups that tapped the SEALs including the CIA and its arms. But then again, there were a lot of decorated soldiers. It didn't always mean they were paramilitary. Her mind went back and forth.

"If it's about this case, I wonder how they got wind of it so fast," her captain mused, reading her thoughts, watching her face.

Claire took off her duty belt and handed it to the captain. She felt bereft as the weight from her belt was taken off her hands. *Should I take a gun up there just in case?* As soon as she thought it, she dismissed the idea. Trust with the hostage-taker was essential.

"Claire, did you hear what I said?"

"About them getting wind of it?" Claire lifted a shoulder. "With NCS, or anything even remotely to do with the CIA, I've learned not to ask questions. You never get a straight answer, anyway." She put the NCS and her father's interest out of her mind as she slipped the vest on over her favorite blue blouse, placing the small microphone so the team could hear the negotiation. Normally she would have protested the Kevlar, but the captain was right. Something was off about this and Claire definitely wanted the extra protection. She wished now, though, that she'd changed her shirt before she headed over here. The Kevlar would more than likely leave wrinkly vest marks and she had plans for later.

"Axis is working with the government somehow, but I can't get a straight answer out of anyone what they're working on exactly. Maybe that's what your father's call is about," Captain Reed said, worry coloring his tone as he bent to help her with the last Velcro strap. "Just watch yourself out there."

Claire nodded. "Don't worry. I don't think he wants to kill his friend. I think it's some sort of PTSD episode." She ran a hand down the vest. "We can do this."

Her captain gave her a hard pat on the shoulder just as an officer came through the glass door to hand her three bottles of water. She held onto them, letting the chill seep through her for a moment. Taking a breath in through her nose and letting it out through her mouth, she envisioned the outcome. Hostage safe, hostage-taker in custody. Everyone fine.

With one last breath in she tried to unravel the knot in her stomach and right then, she was glad she'd worked through lunch. It wouldn't foster any confidence in her abilities if she threw up right before she went out on the roof with a hostage. *I've got this.* With a quick nod to herself and a roll of the water bottles in her hands, she started toward the door that the captain was holding open for her. He looked worried, so she tried to give him a reassuring smile. "I don't think anyone's going to die today if it makes you feel any better."

"Nobody had better," he said under his breath. "Not on my watch."

Claire chuckled softly. "So it's all about your pride then?"

"No, it's all about getting too old for this."

He looked genuinely concerned, which gave Claire pause since the captain was well known for his poker face on operations. "Captain?"

With a wave and a shake of his head, he went back to business. "We'll have you covered. Should Steve try to make contact with him from mobile command?"

"Thanks, but no. Just have him listen and learn on this one." Steve was a quick learner, but he still had a ways to go.

She headed down the hall toward the door to the roof. Pushing through it, she let the door close before she began climbing the concrete stairs, her captain's face running through her mind. *Don't let it spook you,* she told herself firmly. *Focus.*

Claire reached the top and opened the metal door before heading across the roof. With a glance at the sky, she saw the puffy clouds from this morning had turned dark and the breeze was cold. *Please, don't let it rain,* she said silently, sending one more prayer heavenward. That would make a miserable situation even worse.

She smoothed down her ponytail, the wind chasing some loose strands around her face before she could tuck them behind her ear. Running her hands over the condensation from the water bottles, she took a look around, trying to get her immediate bearings. In a short sweep, she could see the rest of the team in her peripheral vision—Bart and Colby to her left and right, respectively, in position on the far sides of the roof and ready to go tactical if needed. It made her feel better seeing them there. They'd been together on the team for so long, they felt like her older brothers.

Straight ahead was her target and she strode toward the two men very near the edge of the roof. Both men were stone-still, watching her. One man was kneeling down, his broad shoulders pulled into a military posture. Crisp. Like he was ready to salute, even though he had a gun to the back of his head, execution-style.

She stopped, suddenly flashing back to the image of her brother kneeling in that same position, the man above him holding a gun to the back of Luke's head while he read a list of demands. Her heartbeat accelerated. *This isn't Luke.* Although the hostage in front of her wore the same expression on his face that her brother had—perfectly calm. He didn't look scared, just *thoughtful.*

Thrown a bit, Claire forced a smile to her lips, even though the tension in her muscles ratcheted up a notch. And while she'd been expecting to possibly see a homemade bomb strapped to Gary, as she got closer, she was surprised to see a sophisticated black ball, a blinking light, and several canisters attached to it peeking out of his halfway zipped, over-sized jacket. Vince's words came unbidden to her mind. *Explosives expert.*

This was obviously worse than she'd thought.

Chapter Three

Rafe watched the woman approaching the edge of the roof, her hands full with three bottles of water, her long brown hair coming loose from her ponytail and flying in her face. She was tall, her arms muscular but feminine, her loose black pants and Kevlar unable to hide her curves. When she paused momentarily, he could see that her face was more square as she set her jaw and started toward them again. Her large eyes definitely assessed the situation as she walked, or rather strode, across the concrete. She was sure of herself. Or wanted him to think she was. *Stay back*, he wanted to shout. But he didn't. He was silent, the gun pointed at the back of his head and the slight clicking of the bomb directly behind him making his tongue thick.

She met his gaze with a reassuring smile before stopping to set the drinks down a few feet away from the edge Rafe was perched on. She held up her hands. "Gary, do you remember we talked on the phone? I'm Claire." She got no response. "How about we enjoy some of this water over here and you can tell me what's going on?"

Gary's voice seemed to be getting weaker by the moment and it made Rafe's stomach twist. The slight clicking started and Gary launched into the rhyme again. When he got to the last line, Rafe closed his eyes. Would this be the time the bomb went off? Would steel balls spray out of those little canisters? Or poisonous gas?

"He can't say anything," Rafe told her, keeping his voice even. "He's as much of a hostage as I am."

Claire lowered her eyebrows. "What do you mean?"

Gary held the phone so Rafe could read the text. "Gary's wired to a modified XM-7 Black Widow. It's cutting edge weaponry. If he doesn't do exactly as he's told, the bomb will detonate."

Rafe watched Claire as she tried to get a look at the bomb under Gary's jacket. Her face registered surprise before her eyes flicked to Gary. Rafe couldn't see any reaction from Claire to the burns and scars that criss-crossed one side of Gary's face. *She's good.* Even though the burns were looking better, Rafe knew Gary kept his brown hair longer, to hide the constant reminder of their last mission together.

Claire took a small step forward, bringing him out of his thoughts. "Is there a way to disarm it?"

"Not that I can see. If I get off my knees or if Gary speaks without permission, they'll detonate the bomb." Rafe ground his jaw, his teeth hurting at the force of his frustration. He felt so helpless, but no matter what, he wasn't going to leave Gary to face this alone.

A strangled sound came from Gary, like he was about to cry. "I'm sorry, man," Rafe told him, turning his head sideways. "I'm going to get us out of this somehow."

Gary started to recite the children's rhyme again, leaning over to show Rafe another text.

"What's going on?" Claire asked. "Is he texting you?"

"The text says they've got a sniper rifle trained on him. If he gives them the encryption key, they'll give him a humane death of being shot instead of blown up," Rafe answered grimly.

"Encryption key for what?" Claire stepped a tiny step closer.

"A file he was working on." Rafe twisted his upper body toward Gary.

"How did you get involved?"

"They texted him to find me and bring me to the roof. Somehow they know we served in the military together. Cowards," he said, his voice rising.

"Do you know who's doing this? Can they hear us?"

Rafe nodded and rolled his neck to the side. "Gary's got a mic taped to him so whoever's doing this can hear everything. Of course they don't have the courage to do this face-to-face." His voice grew louder with each word.

The bomb clicks started and Gary launched into the annoying rhyme. Rafe regretted the day he'd ever laughed over using that line in the field. "Gary, we're going to get out of this, okay? You know me. I can get us out of tough spots. Remember Operation Blackthorn? No one thought we'd come out of there and we proved them wrong. We're still here."

Gary chuckled, the sound pained, but still, it was something and Rafe was glad to hear it. "This is just like a mission. We've got to think strategically." His voice was low and he hoped Gary heard him and not the low-life who'd done this to them. Rafe dropped his chin to his chest. He had to think.

Claire inched closer to them and he lifted his head. *Too close.* "Do you know who's telling you to do this? Can I talk to them?"

Rafe clenched his fist, resisting the urge to push her back from the bomb set to go off right behind him. He didn't know what the payload was in those canisters, but he knew it wouldn't be pretty once it was set off. And he'd seen enough people hurt by bombs to last him a lifetime. Gary showed him the phone with the newest text. "He wants you to take off the Kevlar, Claire. Then he'll talk to you," Rafe told her.

"Can he see us?"

Rafe shrugged. "The Black Widow unit is controlled by a laptop, usually, so he has to be within a thousand foot radius of the bomb." He wished he could stand and assess the situation more clearly, but he didn't want to risk setting the bomber off. Kneeling in the gravel like this had aggravated his knee again and his position gave him a limited view.

Claire tilted her head toward him. "And if I don't take off the Kevlar?"

"I don't think it's a good idea either way," he bit out. "You should go back inside. There's nothing you can do here."

"Can you text them back?" Claire asked Gary, ignoring Rafe's words. Her voice was low and soothing when she talked, like a mother to a child. Rafe was surprised to find it settled him somehow. *Who wouldn't give in to whatever that voice asked for?* He looked up to see her biting her lip at Gary's response. She seemed to have an easy-to-read face and that was a good thing to have in hostage negotiations—open, honest expressions, but eyes that saw everything.

"I don't think I'm going to take off the Kevlar, but I would like to talk to you still. What's your name?"

Gary held the phone down to Rafe. *"Angel of Death. Do you know my work?"*

"I've seen death, if that's what you mean." Claire kept her voice neutral.

"We've all seen death. Too much of it." Rafe's mind was systematically going through any mission or anyone he could think of that could be associated with the name Angel of Death. Nothing popped out to him.

Gary started to recite 'Ring Around the Rosy' again and Rafe closed his eyes. He'd never wanted to hear that rhyme after he'd left Afghanistan. How many times had Gary set munitions then recited it to make sure the team all had a chance to take cover and get to a safe zone before it blew? By the time he'd said *'all fall down'* everyone knew to *get down*. "This has got to be someone in the military, someone we know, Gary," he said, his voice barely audible.

Claire cut in. "What do you mean?"

"Where else would they get that kind of weapon? How would they know that rhyme? None of this is a coincidence," Rafe said.

"What encryption key does he want?"

"All I know is they want an encryption key to a file Gary was working on for the last month. That's what this is all about."

"We don't know any more specifics?" Her voice volume matched his, trying to keep the mic from picking up every word.

Rafe shook his head.

Claire didn't ask any more questions, she just looked thoughtful. "You look like you need a drink of water, Gary. Let me get that for you," she said.

Don't get too close, Rafe thought. The realization that this could go very wrong, very quickly, made every instinct in his body want her away from here, away from them and the bomb, Kevlar or not.

Rafe looked up at Claire, who had stopped in front of them holding three water bottles by their tops. He gave her a half-scowl, but she didn't seem to notice. Instead, she sat down on the concrete, pulling her arms around her knees. At first he couldn't figure out why she'd sit down, but then he realized she was trying to get a better look at the bomb. The wind whipping her hair out of her ponytail was hampering her effort, and even Rafe's tie was starting to flap, but the breeze felt good after being on this hot roof for over an hour. Claire leaned forward and passed one of the drink bottles to him. "Could you hand this to Gary?" she asked, her voice calm, with just a hint of tension.

Without a word, Rafe handed the water bottle back to Gary. He rubbed the water condensation droplets on his neck as he drew his hand back, tilting his head to look at the woman before him, who was watching both of them carefully.

"Can I give a water bottle to Mr. Kelly?" she asked Gary, but her eyes never left Rafe. She didn't wait more than a few seconds for an answer before she just handed Rafe a bottle.

Rafe wanted to sigh with relief, his body grateful since his own throat was so dry it felt like he hadn't had a drink in days. It ached for even a small sip, especially after being in the sun and wind, kneeling on the roof. The pain in his knee was getting intense, the scars straining the skin so tight he knew he couldn't do this much longer. But what choice did he have? The bomber wanted him kneeling in front of Gary. If they didn't obey, they were both dead. So, for now, he knelt.

Rafe reached for the outstretched bottle, quickly twisting off the top to take a sip. His whole being wanted to drink the entire thing, but he took his time. Being in the deserts of Iraq and Afghanistan had taught him a lot about appreciating water. Each sip was like manna from heaven and he savored it.

Gary waited until Rafe was done, then took the empty bottle from him and squatted down, setting it beside them, precisely upright and an inch apart from his own empty bottle. That's how he was-- precise, and that quality had always helped them in the field. "Hang in there, man," Rafe murmured. He was trying to remember everything he'd been told about the XM-7. It was run remotely and disarming it would be difficult—especially with any modifications.

Gary held the phone out to him and for a second Rafe didn't want to look at the text, but he knew he didn't have a choice.

"What does it say?" Claire asked.

"Give me the encryption key and this will all be over." Rafe pressed his lips together. "Gary, what key could possibly be worth your life?"

He was silent until the clicking on the bomb started. That was the signal to say the rhyme again, taunting them with the fact that their lives were in someone else's hands. Gary dutifully said the rhyme, his voice a little more tense, if that was even possible. He got to the final three words and hesitated. *Is that the signal that this is the last time?* "Get back, Claire. Now." But Claire didn't move, merely changed her position to sit on her heels. She wouldn't be able to run

26

from that position. Not that Rafe was any better where he was. They collectively tensed, holding their breath as Gary said the last word.

But nothing happened.

He's toying with us. Rafe's blood pounded in his ears. Gary held the phone down. *LOL,* the text said.

Rafe had had enough. He stood, ignoring his pained knee as much as he could so he could look over the way the bomb was strapped to Gary. If he could jam the signal or take it off this would be over, but Gary stepped back and batted his hand away. "They'll kill us," he hissed, his voice choking on the words. "Kneel back down. I don't want you hurt."

Rafe ignored the command and Claire appeared beside him. "Why don't you give me the phone, Gary? Let me talk to him."

Gary handed her the phone without protest. She took it, but spoke aloud in the direction of Gary's chest, and the mic. "In case you didn't hear earlier, my name is Claire. Can you call me so we can talk this out? Maybe if you tell me what encryption key you want exactly, I could help you."

The phone vibrated and Claire looked at the text. Rafe read it over her shoulder. *"Maybe you should take Gary's place, Claire. Trade your Kevlar for his special vest. Then we'll talk."*

Rafe touched her arm. "No way," he murmured.

Claire pulled away gently. "If I take Gary's place, will you let him and Mr. Kelly go?"

Rafe shook his head. That was never going to happen. When no texts were forthcoming, Gary looked down at the vest, the clicks loud in the silence and he started to recite the rhyme again. "Ring around the rosy, a pocket full of posies, ashes, ashes, we all fall down."

Rafe briefly closed his eyes. Usually the bomb went off right after the word 'down.' It didn't this time, but he knew it was coming. This couldn't go on much longer.

"Tell me what happened exactly, Gary," he growled under his breath, taking a step forward. "We have to get some clues on who's doing this."

Gary was silent until his phone buzzed again. He held it up for Claire and Rafe to see. *Go ahead, tell them.* "I got in my car, I was going to run a few errands during lunch. Someone was in the back seat and they clubbed me. When I came to, I was still in the parking garage, I had the vest and mic on, a text on my phone, and a gun on my chest. The text said to find Rafe in the office and get to the roof. Honestly, that's all I know."

"How did they know you would be here today?" Claire asked Rafe.

He lifted a shoulder. "I have no idea. My brother, Vince, asked me to come down after lunch. So I did."

Gary took a step back. "I'm sorry I got you involved in this, Rafe."

Rafe could feel the tension rolling off Gary as he spoke. "I understand."

"I can't give them the encryption key," he whispered as he rubbed his hand over the mic, trying to muffle his words for anyone listening. "It's a classified file."

Rafe drew his eyebrows together. "Classified?"

"I broke the code and saw what was on the file. It was big. I told Vince about it and he was going to talk to the DoD, get us some protection. Maybe that's why he wanted you to come in." He ran his hand over his face, his fingers tracing the scars on his cheek. He shuffled backwards, a little bit closer to the edge and glanced down. "I don't want to die, Rafe, but I don't want you to die, either."

Rafe saw how dangerously close to the edge he was and knew Gary was starting to think about sacrificing himself. He had to do something before this got out of hand. "We can fix this, Gary. After all we've been through, we're not going to die on this roof!"

Gary was mere inches from the edge now, facing the street below, reciting the rhyme. When he finished he looked back at them. "There's no way out of this. You can't take it off or disarm it. There's a secondary trigger that will go off if anyone tries. They've thought of everything."

"What about the encryption key? Just give it to them. Let the government deal with the fallout. It isn't worth your life."

Gary shook his head. "Thousands of people will get hurt if I give them that key or even say anything about it that will help them get it." He pointed to the mic on his chest. "National security is involved, that's all I can say. And sometimes you've got to sacrifice everything for the good of others."

"Don't be a martyr, Gary," Rafe said, crossing his arms. He felt like he was scolding a small child and it irritated him. "Be specific. Who will be hurt?"

"Do you remember Eagle Claw, Rafe?" Gary's entire body seemed to teeter on the edge as he spoke, the wind pushing and pulling at him, as if it were as undecided as Gary.

"Yeah." Rafe reached for him. "Thanks to you I lived through that one." He pulled on the back of Gary's jacket, for the first time seeing a small trail of blood on his collar from where he'd been hit and knocked out. Anger surged through Rafe's entire body, his fingers curling into fists.

The phone buzzed again and Rafe looked over at Claire. She held it up to him so he could read the text. *"You're in my sights. Give me the key and your friends can live, Mr. Holman. If not, I'll be forced to take action."*

Rafe watched the color drain from Gary's face, then looked at Claire. There had to be something they could do. But what?

The phone was silent, the clicking of the bomb and the wind passing over them the only sounds on the roof now. Gary seemed more agitated than ever, glancing down at the yellow flashing light on

29

the bomb strapped to his chest. He looked back up at the Hartford skyline. "I want you to live, Rafe. I've had your back too many times to fall down on the job now."

Claire put her hands on Rafe and pushed him to the side. Rafe wasn't expecting it and grunted in surprise at her strength. She now stood slightly in front of him, holding her hand out to Gary. Rafe looked at her with a new respect. "I want us all to live. Put the gun down and let me look at the vest. Maybe between the three of us we can do something. Quick. It's our only choice now."

Even the wind seemed to hold its breath for a moment as they all waited for Gary's decision. The clouds finally opened and Gary turned toward Claire, taking a small step away from the edge. He leaned down to slowly put the gun on the concrete, kicking it to the side, reciting the rhyme again as he did so. The raindrops fell softly around them and Rafe stepped close to Claire. Together they moved toward Gary.

They both bent to make an assessment of the bomb and the vest, but Rafe knew it was useless. The secondary trigger made it easy to see if they interfered or touched it in any way, it would detonate. Gary knew it, too. Rafe could see it from the look of realization on his face. Gary's shoulders fell as he raised his face to the sky, his arms outstretched. The blinking yellow light on the top stopped and Rafe's heart sped up, the hair on the back of his neck standing up as if a chill had passed through him.

With rain falling on his cheeks, Gary looked at Rafe. "Don't trust anyone with my file. No one. Not even people you think you can trust. And . . . just remember Eagle Claw." The rain mixed with tears as he took a small step back, just millimeters away from the edge. It was over. Before Rafe could say anything, stop him, apologize—anything—bits of concrete flipped up all around them and gunshots began to ring in his ears.

30

Rafe's military training kicked in and he instinctively reached for his gun. When his hand caught air, he remembered he wasn't carrying any weapons. Crouching down, he looked for cover, reaching out for Gary as he did so. He tried to make himself as small of a target as possible, while bullets rained down on them. The gunman seemed intent on trying to hit all three of them. He needed to run, whether his knee wanted to cooperate or not.

Taking a few steps forward, he knew he was exposed, but he didn't have a choice. Claire was a few feet to his right and he called out to her just as Gary moved in front of him, his body caving inward right before Rafe's eyes. Gary staggered toward Rafe, the blue of his shirt visible above the bomb starting to stain dark as he fell to the ground. "I'm sorry," he gasped.

His sightless eyes stared up at Rafe as he hit the concrete and it was easy to see he was dead. Time seemed to stand still, Rafe's heartbeat the only signal that seconds were still passing. Blood was everywhere and his friend was dead. He started to get up, to go to Gary. *He shouldn't be alone* was all Rafe could think.

"Stay down," Claire shouted to Rafe, grabbing his arm with one hand as she grasped the side of her neck with the other. Before she could move a bullet hit her square in the chest. She dropped to the ground.

Rafe didn't think, he just went into motion, scooping her up to run for the door. The cover fire from the corner of the roof was ratcheting up, giving them time to get clear. Rafe staggered toward the stairs, clutching Claire in his arms. *Not again. Please, God, don't let this happen to me again.*

His thoughts were lost in the explosion behind them and Rafe fell on top of Claire, doing his best to cover her body with his own. Shrapnel ricocheted off the concrete and hit him in the side, the trajectory and the pain of impact knocking the breath out of him. He knew he had to get them both to safety before the gunman finished his job.

Calling upon every reserve of strength he had, he dragged her to a narrow column that offered a modicum of protection. He sagged against it for a moment. Looking down he saw a blood trail down Claire's vest. Rafe started running his hands over her, trying to find the source. "Where are you hit? How many times?" She didn't answer and he felt the panic rise within him. He tamped it down with his years of military training. He willed the calm to come, like a mask falling over him. She wasn't going to die if he could help it.

More spurts of gunfire erupted before she could speak and within moments footsteps thundered toward them. Rafe hugged her body closer to him, wondering if he could make it to the door before the gunman found them and finished them off.

Claire turned her face away and coughed into her shoulder. "Rafe, I can't breathe. You're holding me too tight."

Rafe had never felt so relieved to hear someone speak. She'd seemed so limp just a moment ago. "I saw you get shot. You and Gary." He felt a shudder go through him. "The bomb." He couldn't form a complete sentence. He hugged her again. *She's alive!* He let out a groan of relief.

His relief was short-lived. An olive-skinned man with a sniper rifle appeared suddenly, chewing gum so loudly Rafe could hear it over the thunder of blood rushing through his head. He looked determined to finish his job. Instinctively, Rafe covered Claire with his body once again, feeling the shock hit his system anew.

The gunman tried to pull Claire out from under him, but Rafe clutched her tightly. *No!* He would die before he let anyone else be killed today. He was making his stand, right here, right now.

"Let me take her, man! She's been hit!"

He couldn't release her. It was like if he held her, protected her, then he somehow could redeem himself from the mistakes he'd made. Or maybe if he held her, he wouldn't fall apart himself.

He took a deep breath and Claire looked up at him, her dark eyes taking in every detail of his face. She wriggled an arm between them and touched his cheek. "It's okay," she said softly. "I'm okay."

Rafe's mind cleared as the breeze hit his face and he let her go, his white dress shirt and tie stained with her blood. She needed help, not him. He looked away from his shirt, watching the man quickly throw her over his shoulder before rushing around the corner for the roof exit, while a second man in a bulletproof vest covered them with his high-powered rifle. He shook his head, trying to clear it. These were officers, probably from Claire's team. They were safe. It was over.

The man standing next to him took a defensive position. "You hit?" he asked Rafe.

"I don't think so." But as soon as the words were out of his mouth his side started to throb.

"Let's go." He motioned for Rafe to go behind him while he eyed the building across the street, his rifle at the ready. Rafe obeyed, keeping his face averted from the last place he'd seen Gary. They followed the same path Claire had taken and Rafe quickened his step, still keeping his head down. He used every ounce of self-control he had not to run and find Claire to make sure she was really all right. From the blood drops on the ground, leading to the door, she wasn't as okay as she'd led him to believe.

When they were in the stairwell, the man motioned down the steps. "It's over, man. You made it." His radio crackled and he listened for a moment, then wordlessly started down the stairs. "Come on. There are a lot of people waiting for you."

"Like who?"

"I don't know, man, but I gotta get you down there, okay? Let's keep moving."

Rafe followed him, his eyes glued to the floor, counting the steps between blood drops. It was his fault. This whole thing was his fault. He should have protected Claire, protected Gary. Done something!

Clenching his fist he silently vowed he'd find who did this—even if it took the rest of his life.

Chapter Four

Colby's strong arms picked her up like she was weightless, throwing her over his shoulder and practically running for the exit. She could see Bart moving into a position of cover, his rifle gleaming in the small sliver of sunlight.

"Get Rafe," she instructed. But Colby wasn't listening, he just kept heading toward the door.

"Get Rafe!" she yelled.

"You're hit," he told her quickly as they approached the door. He radioed their position and that he was bringing her to the command center. When he was through checking in, he turned her in his arms so he was cradling her, his breath coming in bursts. "Let Bart take care of Rafe."

Claire closed her eyes, feeling the rain fall gently on her face like tears. "Did we get the shooter?"

"Don't worry about that right now. Stay with me, Claire," Colby commanded. "Open your eyes."

She opened her eyes. A steady trickle of blood dripped down the front of her vest. She bit her cheek, wanting to reassure Colby that she was fine, but all she could do was shiver—from fear, adrenaline or shock, she couldn't tell.

Colby carried her down the stairs and started to wind through the hallways. It seemed like minutes to Claire but was probably only seconds before she was at the now nearly empty command center, where an EMT was waiting. Colby set her in a chair and kneeled in front of her as he started undoing her bulletproof vest. She pushed his hands away. "I can do it myself." She pulled it off, every movement making her chest ache where the bullet had hit her. *If I hadn't been wearing that vest . . .*

"We need to get your wounds checked now."

"I know, Cole. It's okay. The bullet only grazed me. I'm fine." At least that's what she wanted the EMT to say.

She saw Colby give a look to the EMT next to her and she rolled her eyes before giving him her *own* look. "Fine, don't believe me. This guy's going to tell you the exact same thing."

The EMT leaned forward to examine her neck. "Are you sure this is your only injury?" He didn't look her in the eye, just continued to probe around her neck.

She touched her ribcage. "As far as I know."

"It doesn't hurt anywhere else?"

"Yeah, it feels like I got a fastball in the chest. But other than that, no." She looked up at Colby who was standing over them, his arms folded, watching as the EMT checked for broken ribs. His hovering was irritating her. *I'm not a porcelain doll. I'm fine.* "Don't you have something to do? Like go report to the captain or something?"

"No need, I'm right here," Captain Reed said as he strode in. "And somebody better tell me what happened. What were you thinking, Claire? As soon as you saw that bomb you should have turned around and come back down. I think we need to have a talk on what the words 'safe perimeter' mean to you."

"I wasn't about to leave the hostage like that and once I got the texter talking to me I thought maybe we could get that vest off," she said, her voice curt. His assessment rankled. With a glance at her captain's face, though, she took a gentler tone and added, "sir." She ran a hand over her face "What do we know so far?" she asked Colby.

"We know it was a shooter from the building across the street. Looked like a single." Colby started chewing his gum again. He only did that when he was nervous. Today had obviously scared him.

"I'm fine, you know, it's just a flesh wound, that's all." With what she hoped was a reassuring smile, she turned her attention to the captain. "Did you get anything else?"

"As soon as we heard they wanted an encryption key, and DoD had something to do with it, we started trying to reach them. We're also focusing on Gary's computer, obviously, but my priority is finding our shooter. We've got the perimeter exits blocked. He's got to come out sometime." He ran his hand over his head, staring at her. "That was too close, Claire."

She nodded. "I'm fine, sir."

The EMT started to clean and bandage the wound. "So what's the verdict?" the captain asked.

"She's right, the bullet grazed her. There won't even be much of a scar."

"Shouldn't she go home and take it easy?" Colby stepped forward, his eyes on the captain.

"What do you think, Claire? How do you feel?" The captain's voice was solicitous. He was giving her a way out if she couldn't handle any more today.

"No, sir, I'm ready to go back to work. I want to see this through." She tilted her neck so the EMT could more easily apply the bandage. "A few bruises and a graze aren't going to send me home."

Steve poked his head in the door. "Department of Homeland Security is calling. They said it's urgent they speak with you, Captain." He tilted his head to Claire. "Your dad called, too. Personally."

"They can wait." The captain's bark made Steve jump a bit, but he nodded and backed out of the room. The captain looked over at Colby. "Bart take the hostage?"

Colby nodded. "What does Homeland Security want with this?"

"If they heard about the bomb vest, that's pretty obvious. Claire, what do you think?"

"I'm fine." Claire stood up slowly, making sure she didn't wobble. She didn't want to let them see any weakness. Patting her bandage, she took a step forward, but pain shot up her ribs. She gasped and hunched over.

"Sit down." Captain Reed bit out the words. This was an order she had to obey. She sat.

"Stay here. I'll go find Mr. Kelly and we'll get you both in the same room. Then we'll get some questions answered." He moved toward the door. "Do *not* move from that chair until I get back. Colby, make sure of it."

"I don't need a babysitter, sir," Claire said with a frown. "Like I said, I'm fine."

The captain didn't answer, just went through the door, purpose in his step.

Claire tilted her head back carefully, trying to feel the extent of her injury. It had all happened so fast and the adrenaline was still pumping through her system. But even with adrenaline, the side of her body where the bullet had hit the Kevlar was starting to really throb, not to mention the bullet that had narrowly missed hitting her in the carotid artery, leaving her a burning trail across her neck instead. She would be feeling these injuries for a few weeks to come.

Closing her eyes, she tried to recall the last two minutes on the roof. Gary walking toward the edge. The rain starting to fall. Gunfire everywhere. Rafe pulling her body underneath his, his arms tight around her as the bomb went off. She opened her eyes, still feeling his body cocooning her. He'd tried to protect and shield her as best he could, putting his own life in danger. His SEAL training was evident, but she wished she'd been able to do *her* job.

She pushed down her frustration at her apparent ineffectiveness. That scene would play over in her mind again and again until she figured out where she'd gone wrong. Glancing over at Colby who was shamelessly staring at her, she held his gaze, sending him a message that she was fine, even though she knew today was going to take some time for her to mentally process.

Unfortunately, she didn't have any more time to think about it. The captain walked back in, with Bart and Rafe Kelly right behind him.

Rafe's eyes immediately found hers as he moved slowly over to a chair. He sat on the edge, obviously not letting his back touch anything. "Did you hurt your back?" she asked him.

He nodded, his lips a grim line. Opening his mouth as if he were about to say something else, Bart interrupted him to take a seat near her. "How bad's your neck?"

She shook her head. "Just a graze."

The EMT finished packing up his stuff, but looked over at them. "A centimeter to the left and you'd be telling a different story. Or not telling, more likely." He eyed Rafe. "Did you need anything?"

"No, I've already been looked over." Rafe grimaced. "Just some cuts and bruises and a few stitches. I've had worse." He fingered the hole in his left pant leg. "Have they found out anything more? What do we know?"

"We're starting an investigation. From what we heard up there, this is about something Gary was working on. We're looking into that. If you're up to it, I'd like to go back to the beginning. How did this whole thing start?" The captain paced in front of Rafe as he talked and it made Claire want to say sit down. She held her tongue, however.

"I was meeting my brother and had plans to drop in on Gary afterward. I was surprised to see Gary come off the elevator behind me and when I went over to him, I noticed he was really upset. Then I saw the bomb and he told me he was going to the roof. I told the receptionist to call you guys, and I went with him."

"So you don't have any idea who strapped the bomb to him? Colby asked.

Rafe clenched his jaw. "Someone who would kill for an encryption key."

"What's this Eagle Claw that he was talking about? Was that it?"

"I have no idea. Eagle Claw was a mission we carried out as SEALs," Rafe answered.

The captain thought that over for a moment. "Where would he get a bomb like that?" The captain stopped directly in front of Rafe.

Rafe ran a hand through his hair. "I don't know. The last time I saw that sort of weapon, it was in prototype form."

"In Afghanistan, right?" Bart chimed in.

"Yeah, well, that's where I served last," Rafe said, not answering directly.

Claire narrowed her eyes. She knew the type of people who answered questions like that. "Well, we need to know what he was working on. That should give us some answers."

"Do you know why Homeland Security or the CIA would be interested in this besides the obvious?" The captain sat on the edge of the conference table and folded his arms.

"No. It's got to be a company problem. Maybe my brother would know. Or perhaps my father could answer some questions if he's up to it. He's recovering from a stroke." Rafe stood. "If you don't mind, actually, I'd like to go find my brother."

"He's with the investigating officers right now." The captain stood. "I'm sure that's going to take a while."

"We're going to need you to come down to the station and make a formal statement as soon as possible," Claire added.

"Can I come tomorrow morning? I need to go home."

Claire watched him, seeing the tension in his shoulders and face. He'd been through a lot and she didn't want to let him out of her sight. He shouldn't be alone right now.

"The sooner we get the statement, the better your recollection will be," she told him.

He looked her in the face for a long moment. "Believe me, I won't forget any second of this afternoon for a very long time."

The haunted look in his eyes was one *she* wouldn't forget for a very long time. Claire's heart ached for him. "It shouldn't take long at the station, I promise."

He shifted his long legs into another position, clasping his fingers tightly in his lap. He was in pain and it was obvious he didn't want to be here. Claire's eyes moved to his face, which was inscrutable now, a business-like mask. He was good at hiding his true feelings, she decided. Must've had a lot of practice.

"Let's go," Claire slowly stood, holding her side. "The sooner we get this over with, the sooner Mr. Kelly can go home."

"Are you okay? You look like you're going to pass out," Colby said, walking to her side. "Do you want me to call the EMT back?"

"No," Claire said quickly, stepping away. "Colby, really, don't make me say it again. I'm *fine*."

"We should probably both get checked out at the hospital." Rafe's words were clipped.

"After we get your statement," she said, using her let's-be-reasonable tone as she waited for him to stand. She followed him to the door.

41

Colby was right on her heels. "I'll go with you."

Bart silently stood up as well until they were a misshapen cluster with Claire in the middle. "Might as well get the paperwork started."

The captain peered up at them all. "I'll meet you there when I'm finished here." He stood and opened the door. "When you're done with the statement I want you to go home. Take the rest of the day off. That's an order."

Claire nodded meekly and went through the open door, with Rafe in front of her, and Colby and Bart right behind. "Vince was told to go to the mobile unit. We can see if the officers still have him there."

Colby stepped to her side. "Why don't I go get the car and pull it around?"

Claire resisted the urge to roll her eyes. "Stop it, right now, Cole."

"Stop what? Caring that you got shot today?" He moved past Rafe who was a few steps in front of them. "You should just bring Vince down to the station as well. We can question them together."

Watching him go, Claire realized Rafe had turned around and was observing her, his eyes narrowed. He just stood there in the darkened hallway, his stance alert and cautious, as if he was expecting something else to happen to her. *What's with everyone today? I'm still standing.*

Even as she thought it, she felt unsteady walking toward Rafe. Pushing her shoulders back, she concentrated on putting one foot in front of the other. When she reached Rafe he turned so they could walk side by side, but his frame made the hallway seem smaller than normal. She took a longer step forward to give herself some space, but just as she did so, she felt a shooting pain go through her chest and side. Putting her hand on the wall to steady herself, she ground her teeth together and slowed, hoping Rafe hadn't noticed. She knew he had the second he put his hand on her elbow.

"You okay?" he murmured softly near her ear.

"Yeah," she said, but her side felt anything but fine. "I've got a pretty good bruise from that bullet I took earlier." His hand tensed on her for a moment before he let go and she was sorry she'd said it so bluntly. "It wasn't your fault, Rafe. None of this was your fault."

He didn't reply, just stared straight ahead.

Bart came up beside them. "You know, I think Cole's right. Why don't we just have Vince brought to the station? Then you can get a change of clothes, Claire, and something to eat."

The more she walked, the more her body ached, so she nodded quickly at Bart's words. "Good idea. I'll go with Colby and Rafe. You go with Vince."

Claire picked up the pace. The sooner they could figure this out, the sooner both she and Rafe could find some closure to what had happened on that roof. The memory of her last glimpse of Gary's face before the shooting started flashed through her mind. *How could it have ended that way? Why?*

They endured a silent elevator ride. Claire picked up the pace as she walked through Axis's front glass doors, now flanked by Rafe and Bart. She was still on alert, her eyes scanning the crowd in front of them as she kept Rafe close to her side. Wordlessly, they glanced at the swarm of onlookers, reporters, and emergency personnel held back by barricades. Bart broke off halfway to the car to get to the mobile unit. "See you there," he said over his shoulder, not waiting for a reply.

I would have thought the rain might thin the crowd, she thought. But it hadn't. Claire watched Bart disappear in the throng. She subconsciously touched her new bandage at her neck, quickly pulling the elastic band out of what was left of her ponytail to haphazardly arrange her hair over the bandage. Eyes forward, she concentrated on navigating her steps to the car with the least amount of pain to her chest.

Breathing a sigh of relief as Colby pulled up, Claire immediately went around to the driver's side. Colby was already shaking his head. "You're not going to drive. You were shot today and lost blood."

"I'm fine." She reached for the door handle again, wanting to feel that small moment of control, even if it was just driving a car, but Colby wouldn't hear of it. He got out, took her arm and escorted her to the passenger side.

"No, Claire." He opened the door for her.

Giving him a look of frustration, she got in and glanced over at Rafe reaching for the rear passenger door behind the driver. Colby slid into the driver's seat beside her and gave her a grin as he started the car. She held in a smile at Colby's protectiveness. He had her back no matter what and she was grateful for it, even if it was annoying sometimes.

When everyone was inside, with seatbelts buckled, he pulled the car into drive and headed back to their second home.

"Well, the good news is Homeland Security and the NCS are interested in this one. Maybe they'll take it off our hands," Colby said conversationally.

"No, I want this one," Claire said. She glanced back at Rafe. "There's more to this than we're seeing." Rafe had tilted his head back and closed his eyes. The dark smudges underneath his eyes spoke to the fact that he hadn't slept much recently. *Nightmares from his time in Afghanistan?* If that was the case, today wouldn't help any.

Colby pursed his lips and stepped on the accelerator, squealing the tires as they made a turn. Claire barely missed being slammed into her door. She grabbed her ribs and stifled a yelp of pain. "What are you doing?" Claire asked, not able to keep the anger out of her voice. Turning around she saw Rafe trying to right himself, gingerly touching his knee.

"Sorry," Colby said, his hands clenched on the wheel. "I didn't mean to take it so fast. I'm just wondering what *you're* doing. You've got enough cases on your desk to last you to the next decade without taking this on, Detective. Or have you forgotten your day job?" He lowered his voice even further, a hard edge creeping into his tone. "You were almost killed today, Claire. You don't need this."

"I think I'm the best judge of what I need," she said, matching her tone to his. "I'm okay."

"If you say so," he murmured, nearing the station now.

Claire was caught off-guard by Colby's demeanor and tried to shrug it off. She'd pin him down later on what this was *really* about. "You okay?" she asked Rafe, briefly turning her chin toward him.

"Yeah." He didn't look at her, just kept his face toward the window, his jaw clenched.

Should we take him to the hospital? Claire let that mull through her mind, thinking of what she could say to keep him talking so she could make a better assessment. "How did you hurt your knee? Your brother said you were on leave for a knee injury."

"Some insurgents surprised us. I was up on the mountainside trying to get to the extraction point. I went down."

"At least you made it out alive." Her brother Luke's face flashed before her eyes. He hadn't been so lucky.

"How long have you worked in hostage negotiations?" Rafe finally asked, obviously changing the subject.

Claire glanced over at Colby who sat with that grim look still on his face. "I've been doing hostage negotiation with the team for about three years," she replied. "I've been on the force for eight. In my day job, I'm a detective."

"Sounds stressful. Dangerous. Especially for someone—well," he hesitated, then continued, "for a woman."

45

Claire felt the familiar defensiveness at being judged by her gender rise up. "Doing my job has nothing to do with being a woman."

"I meant no offense," Rafe said quickly, as he leaned forward to catch her eye. "I'd just like to hear your story sometime, why you chose this for a profession."

Taking in a little breath, Claire forced a smile and tried to change the subject herself. That was a story she wouldn't be telling anytime soon. Too complicated. "Well, a job like this is a team effort and I have great backup."

Colby maneuvered into his regular parking spot of the police station. Claire had never been so grateful to get out of a small confined space, the overprotective attitude radiating from Colby combined with awkward conversation topics with Rafe made her uncomfortable. "Here we are." She undid her seatbelt and stepped out of the car.

Colby matched her movements and grabbed her as soon as she was within his reach. "What's your plan? We're just taking a statement, right?"

"Right." Gary's face flashed into her mind once more, making her fists clench reflexively. She wanted to do more than take a statement. "Well, maybe I want to work this one a bit, see where it goes. I can't accept how it went down." Claire's fingers stole to the bandage on her neck. "I just need to do this, okay?"

Colby nodded, still a little hesitant. "Just take things easy, Claire. You've got a lot on your plate right now."

Letting out a breath, she frowned. "What's going on? You've never treated me like I was made of glass before, Cole. I can handle this."

"You've never been shot before." Colby locked her in a staring contest as Rafe joined them, but no one said anything for a long moment.

"Shall we?" Rafe finally asked, breaking the silence and gesturing toward the building with his arm. "After you."

Claire took a deep breath and walked into the station. The lobby was the same. She walked through it, the hall to the offices just as it was when she'd left. The flooring was the same, the walls were the same. All the desks were in the same spots, the people just as busy. Yet, everything was different. *Everything?* No, just one thing. Her.

She was going to work this case, no matter what. She already had enough regrets in her life. This wasn't going to be another one.

Chapter Five

Rafe was tired and hurting. He wanted to go home, but knew he owed it to Gary to do everything he could to find his killer. Following Claire through the door of the station, they walked down a long hall that opened up into a small row of cubicles. Claire ducked into one and Colby went to his a few feet away. Rafe decided to stick with Claire. Approaching her desk, he sat down in the chair near the entrance, while she sat in her swivel chair, wiggling her mouse to wake up her computer. "I'll take you to the interview room in a moment. I just wanted to print something off."

"Okay." He looked around her "office." Neat. Not a lot of knickknacks.

After staring at her screen for a moment longer, she stood. "Follow me, please."

She grabbed a paper out of the printer that was on their way, then they walked further down the hall until she opened the door to a small room. "Have a seat." She closed the door behind them. "As you probably already know, this will be videotaped."

Claire sat down and pointed toward the other chair in the room. She stated her name, his name, the date and time of the interview. "Okay. Let's start with the moment you saw Gary come into the office today. Even the smallest detail can help so don't leave anything out."

Rafe was grateful she wasn't doing a third degree routine. Going over the events of today in detail would help him focus on the process instead of the emotion so he could strategize his next move, find some clues to Gary's killer. He was going to do something, he just didn't know what yet—only she didn't need to know that.

He started going over what had happened. Claire sat in silence, staring at him. It was like she could see right through him. He shifted in his seat, returning her gaze. Her eyes were still guarded, he noticed, and the expression on her face made him wonder what she was thinking. He didn't have to wonder for long. The third degree started.

"So what about Eagle Claw? It seemed to have a lot of meaning for Gary."

Rafe looked down at the table. "It was a search and capture mission. We retrieved the target and were heading for extraction when insurgents started coming out of every crevice on the mountainside. We were in the firefight of our lives, I'll tell you. I was wounded and fell back. Gary came for me. He always had a back up plan and he got us out of there."

"Who was the target?"

Rafe knew he couldn't tell her that, so he simply gave the answer he'd given since he'd come home from the war. "It's classified."

"Classified." She bent over her paperwork, scribbling down a note. "Was there anything unusual about Eagle Claw?"

"No, not really." His mind went over the mission. They were surprised by the insurgents. Gary had made a fallback plan to get to the extraction point. He was always over-preparing. Is that what he was trying to tell Rafe? That he had a back up for the files?

Claire was quiet for a few moments, and Rafe was grateful for the silence as his thoughts swirled through him. When he looked up, however, he noticed she had clenched her hands together and they were trembling slightly. "Are you okay?" he asked gently. "Maybe you should take Colby's advice and go home. We can start this again tomorrow."

"Best advice I ever heard," Colby said as he entered the room. He handed Claire a bottle of orange juice. "Get some juice in you, if you're going to be stubborn about this. The adrenaline will wear off, you'll need some pain meds, and you'll be glad you had something in your stomach." He leaned over her desk. "No arguments."

Claire smiled, any trace of uncertainty erased as she popped the top off. "You won't get any arguments from me." She took a long pull from the bottle. "Thanks, Cole."

Rafe couldn't take his eyes from her. The way she smiled lit up her whole face. He wondered what was between her and Colby. From the look of things, Colby was pretty protective. He glanced down at the bloodstains on her blouse and felt protectiveness surge in him as well. She took another sip of her drink, her hand brushing the stark white bandage on her neck—a reminder of how close she'd come to death today. The thought made his chest tighten.

She looked up and found both men watching her. "What? Do I have some dirt on my chin or something?"

Colby turned away to grab a chair and sat down next to Rafe. "Just finish it off," he growled good-naturedly.

Rafe watched the exchange between them. "How long have you two worked together?"

"Colby was here when I got here," she told him.

"We make a good team," Colby agreed. "Now that I've taught you everything I know."

Claire snorted. "That wasn't much, my friend. I think we covered all of your expert knowledge before lunchtime my first day."

51

Rafe watched with interest as Colby's eyebrows drew down with her use of the word 'friend.' *Interesting.*

"What? Did you think of something?" Claire asked Rafe, pulling him out of his thoughts.

"Not really. Just thinking about today." He folded his arms, trying to cover just how closely he'd been watching her.

"Oh, it looked like you might have remembered something."

Rafe crossed his legs, keeping steady eye contact with Claire. "No. I've told you all I know. I need to talk to Vince. Any news on when he'll be here?"

"Should be any minute now." Claire picked up a pen and tapped it against the edge of the table. "Can you go over it one more time? There's got to be something we're missing."

"There isn't anything else. Honestly." Rafe looked down at his bloody shirt. He felt grimy, his face and hands dirty and wind-chapped. He stood slowly. "Do you mind if I take a break? The EMT gave me a little wipe to clean up with, but I really want to wash up somewhere."

Claire pushed her chair back. "I'm sorry I didn't think of that sooner. I was anxious to get going on the case."

She's standing up pretty slowly, he thought observing the tiny grimace on her face at the effort. *She's still hurting.*

"The men's room is down the hall. I'm going to go make a few phone calls so don't worry if I'm not here when you get back. Just wait for me."

Rafe nodded, his knee protesting at the thought of more walking, but the need to get some of today off him was greater.

"I know you think you're hiding how much pain you're in, but I do try to read people for a living." Claire drew her eyebrows together. "You may need to go to the hospital after all."

"Look who's talking," he said, with a snort. "I'll go if you go."

Colby came to stand next to Claire, looking as if he was waiting to catch her if she fell or something. From the glower he gave Rafe it was obvious he didn't think much of him. *Whatever.*

"I need to talk to you." Colby took her elbow and led her to the door, leaving it open for Rafe. Their voices faded as they walked down the hall, but he could tell from the tone that whatever Colby wanted to talk to her about, Claire didn't want to listen.

With a sigh, he left, following Claire's directions to the men's room. Opening the door, he let it close behind him before he walked to the sink. He leaned over the porcelain, staring at himself in the mirror. The same face he'd looked at this morning was there, but it was dirtier and looked older somehow. He'd missed a large smear of blood near his chin. Was it his? Gary's? Claire's? When he couldn't bear to look any longer, he reached down to turn on the faucet, splashing his face with cold water. It felt good, the biting cold raking his chin and cheeks.

He scrubbed harder, wishing he had a shower, but feeling a bit better just having a clean face free of dirt and blood. Inside, however, he knew the emotional wounds from today would take much longer to fade, if they ever did. Losing Gary was like having a piece of his heart ripped out. They'd been through so much together.

Without another glance in the mirror, he made his way back to Claire's office, bypassing the interview room. Sitting down at Claire's desk, he picked up the pen, then put it down again. If Gary had an encryption key, where would he keep it? Probably in the server room. He remembered Gary showing him the little corner he'd fixed up for himself when he wanted to be alone. Maybe he'd put it there?

"Forget where you're supposed to be?" Colby leaned up against the corner of the cubicle entrance.

Rafe immediately straightened in his chair. "No, I just need a few minutes, thanks."

"Hmmm . . . Claire should be right back. Don't touch anything." He said before walking away.

Rafe ignored Colby's command and picked up Claire's phone. He pressed Vince's cell number. He picked up after two rings, but Rafe could barely hear his 'hello.' "Are you still at the office?" Rafe asked. "What's all that noise? I thought you were on your way here."

"I'm still in the lab. These government guys want access to everything Gary worked on," Vince's voice was fading in and out.

A sliver of alarm went through Rafe at Vince's words since Gary had been very specific not to trust anyone. "Who's with you? Is Bart there?"

"Rafe, you're cutting out. What did you say?"

"I'm coming back to the office. Stay right there."

The call was cut off. He put the phone down, his gut twisting. Who was with him? If Gary had died guarding his work, Vince didn't realize the danger he was in. Rafe had to get back to the office, if nothing else just to escort Vince home, until they knew more about Gary's murder. Running his hand through his hair, he made another call, to the company's driver with directions on where to pick him up. He didn't normally use company resources, but he knew Vince would want to go home in that car no matter what so Rafe might as well have it ready to go.

He stood, resisting the urge to pace. The driver would be here in ten minutes. Clenching his fist, he tried to push away his frustration. *Keep it together*, he told himself.

"Pain get any worse?" Claire's voice came from behind him and it took all of Rafe's self-control not to jump.

"Not really. Just wondering why Vince is being kept on-site when you said he would be on his way here. Do we know who's with him? Is it Bart?"

"I haven't heard anything about Vince yet. We did find the sniper's nest across the street in the next building over. They're collecting evidence now."

Rafe shook his head. "This guy was a professional. There's no way he would have left anything behind."

Claire gave him a curious look. "Well, it can't hurt to try. Maybe we'll get lucky." She gently touched his shoulder as she came around the desk and sat down. "Bart should be escorting Vince here soon. I promise. We're trying to be thorough and figure out why Gary was killed. You can trust me you know. I'm not playing games."

Rafe decided to take her at her word. For now. "I just talked to Vince who said the guy with him is trying to gain access to all of Gary's files."

"I'm sure they're trying to gather information to help the investigation."

Rafe let that sink in. Something was wrong. He couldn't explain how he knew.

Colby poked his head in before Rafe could say anything else. "Claire, Will's here for you. Waiting at the front desk."

Claire looked at her watch. "Gah! I was supposed to meet him. I forgot." She looked down at her blouse. "I need a minute to change. Can you stall him?"

Colby nodded and disappeared down the hall. "I'm sorry, but this is important, I've put him off twice already this week. If I do it again—well, I can't," she told Rafe. "I'll make it quick. If you could sit here and finish your statement with Colby, I'll be back before you're done. Then we can all go through the process when Vince is here."

This is my way out. Rafe shook his head. "I'll have to come back tomorrow. I need to get back to the office." He used his professional, this-is-what's-going-to-happen voice. It was rare anyone questioned him when he used that tone.

"Rafe, the office building is a crime scene right now. There's nothing you can do there. And I hate to pull rank on you, so I'm asking you nicely to sit down and finish your statement. I won't babysit you, but you know this is going to get done one way or another. Then I'd be happy to escort you back to the office if you still want to go." Her voice was just as businesslike as his and she even said it with a smile on her face. *She's good.*

Rafe shook his head. He didn't want her to think he was questioning the police capabilities, but he knew he needed to get back to his brother. As soon as possible. "I'm sorry, I want to help, but I need to get back to Axis. If you really think it's necessary, I can probably come back in an hour or two. I don't want you to have to worry about hurrying back from a date with your husband."

Claire looked over at him, her eyes narrowed. "It's not my husband, it's my half-brother," she corrected. "He's having some troubles and my stepmother thought I could talk to him so I was going to meet him at the diner down the street." She grabbed her purse and started rifling through it. "Like I said, I can't cancel, but I'll cut it short. He understands things come up in my job. So you'll stay and finish your statement?"

Rafe stood. "Sure." He would finish writing quickly and add more details tomorrow, but she didn't have to know that. "So you have a brother? How old is he?"

"Sixteen."

With a nod, he leaned his hip on the desk, careful of his knee. "In a bit of trouble?"

She was still looking for something in her purse and didn't look up, just murmured an mmhmm.

"My family has season tickets to the Connecticut Whale games. If he likes hockey, that is." Claire finally looked up at him as he spoke, her eyes questioning. "I know the coach and sometimes I can go back in the locker room and hang out with the players. I'd be happy to introduce your brother." He backed up a bit, trying to gauge her reaction. "If you want. Sometimes it helps teenagers if they have some sort of incentive," he trailed off. "I feel like I owe you something after today."

"You don't. But since he does love hockey, maybe I'll mention it to him," was all she said as she zipped up her purse again.

Rafe tried to keep his reaction casual, realizing it felt good to offer something nice to her and her brother after the horror of today. "Okay," he said with a shrug, not wanting to push it. He caught her arm as she went by, making sure he didn't jostle her too much since it was on the same side as her neck wound. "You know, I don't think you should drive. Colby was right about that. Let me take you. Or call the company's service."

"You have a service?" Claire said, surprise in her voice.

"It picks up clients from the airport, giving them a driver in the city. It's a convenience, that's all." Rafe kept his voice even. "And it's already on its way."

Claire smiled. "Well, lucky for you, I don't need to drive. Like I said, it's just down the street. I just don't want Will to see the blood . . ." She gestured to the stains on her blouse, her countenance falling. It was obvious she was thinking about how that blood got there. After a moment she recovered and met Rafe's eyes. "I have to go change. I'll be right back." She turned and walked down the hall. "See you in a few."

Rafe sat down, the image of her being shot right in front of him still vivid in his mind. He was grateful she was alive. Watching her walk away, that rush of protectiveness rose up in him again and he almost stood and went after her. *She can take care of herself. She doesn't need me.*

He heard her call to Colby, "See you later. Tell the captain I'll be back shortly," and then she was gone.

Rafe scribbled a few more sentences, including his cell phone number, keeping his word to finish his statement. He stood, trying to take a step without limping noticeably. His knee was really starting to seize up with each movement and the little bit of local he'd been given for the gash in his back was wearing off. He knew he probably wouldn't be able to stay on his feet much longer without some pain meds. He started for the door and was just a few feet away when Colby called out. "Hey, where are you headed?"

"I'll be right back," he said over his shoulder.

Rafe thought Colby might question him further, but he didn't. Rafe walked slowly to the parking lot, seeing Claire and a boy just taller than her stop at a navy blue Mazda. She opened the passenger door and threw in a small bundle of fabric, probably her blouse, before walking down the street. Rafe noticed she walked like she was a little more relaxed, now dressed in a light gray sweater instead of the bloodstained blue blouse. He watched for a moment before going around the corner to the pre-arranged spot where the driver would pick him up.

The driver appeared in the Mercedes and quickly pulled in front of him. He climbed into the back and sank into the soft leather seat. It was all he could do not to sigh in pleasure. He wished he could make a detour and head home to Glastonbury for a quick shower and change of clothes, but he felt an urgency to get back to the office, to find Vince and then strategize a plan.

They pulled into the parking garage in record time and Rafe thanked the driver. "Wait out front for Vince, I'll take my own car from here," he told him. "Thanks so much for coming for me." The driver nodded and drove away.

Rafe walked through the parking level, making sure his car was still near the entrance a few rows over. He glanced at the entry door in front of him, grateful now his father had chosen the specific corner office that had a private elevator, so he could have that luxury.

It was the only way in Rafe had now, since he couldn't get past lobby security without a badge and he didn't want to get stopped by the cops who were there. He just needed to find Vince. Quickly pressing the elevator button, he stepped inside.

The elevator doors whooshed shut and the hairs on Rafe's neck prickled. As he ascended, he suddenly had a feeling of foreboding start in his stomach. "Settle down," he told himself. "You'll find him."

The elevator stopped, the doors slid open and for the second time that day, Rafe found himself looking down the barrel of a gun.

"I've been expecting you, Mr. Kelly."

Chapter Six

Claire quickly checked her appearance in the window before they went into the diner. Fluffing out the parts of her hair that had gone flat in the rain, she tried to arrange it over her neck, so as to best hide her bandage. She didn't want Will to worry.

She walked next to her brother who had suddenly gotten taller than her. He was still a little gangly, but was starting to fill out. It made her realize she hadn't seen him enough these past months. Things were changing and passing her by.

Will gave her a look, his thick brows drawn together, his hands in his over-sized jacket. She nudged him. "Hey, what's that look for?"

"Nothing," he said, but his eyes didn't meet hers. Instead he went over to their favorite booth and sat down. "Don't you ever get sick of eating here?"

Claire laughed. "If I didn't eat here, I'd probably starve. They're the closest place to the station."

Claire sat down across from him, watching Will shrug out of his jacket and throw it on the seat. She quickly looked down to cover her surprise at the change in Will. He was wearing a t-shirt with a skull on it and his baggy jeans looked like they might fall off at any moment. *Hasn't it only been a couple of weeks since I've seen him?* Looking at him today, it felt much longer. He flipped the hair out of his eyes to give her a resentful look.

"I know Mom told you to take me out and talk to me, but I don't need you nagging me, too. I get enough of it from her."

Well this wasn't exactly how I imagined this starting out, she thought. "I'm not going to nag you, Will. It's just been a while since I've seen you and I wanted to catch up."

"You haven't stopped by in weeks and you never have time for me anymore. Even when we make plans you cancel." He turned to eye the exit as if she was going to disappear right that second.

Claire drew a breath. Had it been that long? "I'm sorry, Will. I know things have been hard for you."

"Why did Dad have to take that job when he knew he would have to move back to Washington? He's breaking my mom's heart. All she does now is cry and wait by the phone for him to call. It's obvious he never really loved us." He glared at her, daring her to contradict him.

"He loves you," Claire said softly, reaching across the table. "He always says how proud he is of you."

He let her touch his hand for a moment before drawing back. "I'm not Luke. He's proud of Luke and loves *him.* That's why he asks me why I can't be more like my older brother."

"You and Luke are totally different people."

"If he loves me so much, why'd he leave then? Why is it all about his job? He could have retired." Will kept his eyes looking downward.

"Will, your parents are trying to figure out their marriage. Your mom stayed here so you could finish school and be close to your grandma. You know that." Claire sighed.

"Yeah, right. He got us all settled here, then as soon as Washington snaps their fingers with a higher salary and a title, he's right back there."

"Dad felt like he couldn't pass up being chief since he's worked for it his whole life, but he wants to make it work with his family, I know he does. Sometimes it's just hard." She was surprised she could say that without a bitter tone. "Just because he isn't here doesn't mean he loves us any less. He's busy keeping the country safe."

She didn't mention that her dad's job had killed his marriage to her mother as well. Balancing family with a government job was not her dad's strong suit and it was happening all over again, only she was an adult, watching another kid go through it. At least she'd had Luke to lean on then. *Why did Dad do this again?* "We just have to be patient."

"Why should I be patient? He left. He doesn't care. He's only called me a few times. Has he called you?"

Claire thought of the phone calls she'd received today. That had been their only contact for a month or more. *I wonder if it's about Gary's case.* "A couple of times. It's hard for him. There are a lot of international things going on right now. I'm sure he'll call every chance he gets. He cares about us."

"He *cares* about us, but he *loves* his job."

Claire could see the anger and grief manifest in every look and gesture. It was as if she were looking at herself as a teenager. "I want things to work out just as badly as you do. We're all doing our best I think."

Claire sighed, memories of her own childhood making her eyes prick. Her older brother Luke had made the absence of her father hurt less. Will didn't have anyone except her for that. "I'm here for you Will. Anytime, you know that."

Will looked up then, the anger taking over. "Okay, sure. I have to make an appointment to see you and I bet you have to get right back to the office, don't you?" When she didn't answer, he shook his head. "I knew it. What's the point to my life? Nobody even wants me."

Biting her lip, Claire felt the tears begin to fall and blur her vision, feeling every inch a failure as a sister. "*I* want you. Your mom wants you. Dad wants you. It's just hard right now." She reached over and grasped his arm. "I'm sorry, Will. I really am. I'll try to do better." She discreetly wiped her cheeks. "You're the only brother I've got left."

The waitress appeared at her elbow and Claire quickly looked down, wishing they could have had one more moment of privacy. "Hi, I'm Sherrie and I'll be your waitress today. Can I bring you something to drink?" the woman asked.

"Just ice water, please," Claire told her, looking across at Will.

"Coke for me, Sherrie," Will said as he smiled for the first time since Claire had arrived. She looked up at the waitress and saw why his attitude had changed so quickly. She was young, maybe early twenties, with red spiky hair and a nice smile. Probably new, since Claire hadn't seen her here before.

She wrote down what they said and leaned forward to gesture toward their menus with her pen. "Do you need a few more minutes?"

Will sat up straighter and opened his menu. "What do you recommend?" he asked, nodding at the specials. "Are any of these good?"

Claire hid a smile, watching Will scoot closer to the edge so Sherrie could lean over even further to point to a special in the middle and extol its virtues. The kid was good, she had to admit. He probably had that menu memorized with as often as he'd eaten here, yet he had the waitress thinking it was his first time.

When Sherrie was gone, Claire leaned over the table. "She's cute."

"She is *hot*," Will said, craning his neck a bit to try to catch a glimpse of her.

"I think she's a little old for you."

"I'll be seventeen in a couple of months. Maybe she likes younger men."

"She'd be lucky to have you. When you're older, maybe." Claire unwrapped her napkin and took out her knife and fork. "So what's this I hear about you cutting class?"

Will looked away. "Got something better to do than sit in class and listen to some old guy drone on. It's all stuff I don't care about."

"You're failing, Will. How do you expect to get into college if you flunk out?"

"I'm not going to college," he said, his eyes defiant. "There's no reason to."

"But you always planned on being a lawyer, or joining the service. It's all I've heard you talk about since you were in grade school."

"Well, things change."

Claire sighed again. "Will, I'm worried about you. Things don't change that much in so short a time. I hardly recognize you. Your hair is long, you don't care about school, and let's just say I bet you're not wearing the sweater I got you for Christmas." The nice pullover she'd chosen definitely didn't seem to fit his current style. Her voice trailed off. "Tell me what I can do."

She watched Will's face, the emotions running across it as she talked. This was a lot worse than she'd thought. Guilt washed over her. She should have been there for him.

"There's nothing to do," he said finally. "I'm just figuring things out."

"Why don't we make some plans," she offered. "Let's ask your mom if we can go out to the late movie tonight or something. We haven't had a family movie night in a long time."

For a second his face brightened, but then fell. "She won't go. She doesn't leave the house anymore except for work. She just sits by the stupid phone waiting for Dad to call."

"Well, it sounds like she needs a night out." Claire took out her phone. "Let me call her." She looked down at her cell and realized she had three missed calls. Pressing the button to view, she was a little surprised to see her dad's personal number. Knowing a call to her dad probably wouldn't go over well with the angry Will she had in front of her right now, she went ahead and dialed her stepmother. She watched the flicker of hope in Will's eyes as she put the phone to her ear, but as it rang and rang, that flicker died. "Voice mail," she said finally, before she hung up. "We could still go. I don't have any plans tonight."

"Yeah, right," he said sarcastically. "Let's just eat before you have to run out of here."

Sherrie appeared again with their food and they both relaxed in companionable silence as they ate. Claire tried to ask a few questions to get a conversation going, but Will wasn't really in the mood to talk until she brushed her hair over her shoulder. "What happened to your neck?" he asked.

"Nothing," she said, quickly covering it again.

"Nice double standard," he said. "I have to do all the talking, but you don't have to say a word?"

"It's just a graze," she said finally, quickly taking another bite.

"You got shot!" he answered, his voice incredulous. He leaned over and pulled her hair back. "When did this happen?"

"About an hour before I met up with you."

Will sat back in his seat, silent for a moment. "So you got shot at work, then came here to meet me. That's why you were late?"

"Yes."

He let this sink in for a moment. "Did you go to the hospital?"

"I was treated on scene."

"Do you know who did it?"

"No."

Will looked around as if the shooter could be in the restaurant. "So how did it happen then?"

"If I tell you, you have to tell me the real reason why you're cutting class." She folded her arms for emphasis.

"Okay, deal."

"It was a hostage negotiation." She raised her eyebrows. "So why are you cutting class?"

"No way, I need more than that if you want me to tell you anything. Did the guy with the hostage shoot you?" He took a long drink, his eyes never leaving hers.

He's just as stubborn as always. Claire shook her head. "Okay. No, it wasn't the guy with the hostage. I was still working to get him out of the situation, when someone from the building across the way started shooting. We're still working on finding the shooter."

"Why did he take a hostage?"

Thinking of how best to describe it without too many details, she finally settled on, "We don't really know yet." She sipped her water. "Any other questions?"

"How's the hostage? Did he survive?"

Rafe's face flashed through her mind, even though he wasn't exactly the hostage. *I wonder how he's coming with his statement. I need to get back.* "Yeah, he made it out just fine."

Will stared at her for about a minute until she couldn't take it anymore. "What?"

"Nothing," he said, with a familiar grin. "I'm glad you weren't hurt worse. And that you still came."

"Me, too," she said, finally feeling like the ice had melted between them. She'd be better about keeping in touch. That was a promise to herself. "You know, the guy was so grateful that neither of us were killed, he offered to let me take you to a Connecticut Whale game and introduce you to the players."

The memory of the uncertainty in his eyes as Rafe had mentioned it rose to her mind. *I feel like I owe you,* he'd said.

"He'd introduce me to the players?" Will's whole face lit up. "Did you say yes?"

"I said I'd ask you." She smiled at the look on his face. "So, should I tell him yes?"

"Definitely," he told her. "They have a game tomorrow night."

"I don't know. That might be a little soon. He was injured today. He might need a week or two to recuperate."

"Oh," Will said as he sat back. "Okay. I'll look up the schedule online when I get home."

For the first time all day, the old Will she'd loved since the day he was born surfaced, and Claire felt a surge of those same feelings for the boy in front of her. "I'll give him a call and let him know we're definitely interested."

Sherrie came and offered them dessert. Claire declined, but Will asked for a piece of pie to go. "I'll have it waiting by the door," Sherrie said.

Getting up to leave, Claire touched Will's arm. "Okay, so I talked. Now it's your turn. Why are you cutting class?"

"I've been going to Jake's to play *Call of Duty,*" he said as he turned his face away.

"You're cutting class for a video game?" *He wants attention.* Her formerly straight-A brother would never do this. She sighed, deciding to use Rafe's offer as a negotiating incentive. "Okay, how about we make a deal. I will take you to meet the Whale players if you don't cut class the rest of the term. Not even once."

Claire turned to see where Will's attention had gone. He was very busy watching Sherrie walk away, her black skirt brushing the back of her knees. "Did you say something?" he said absently.

Claire hit him on the arm. "Yeah, I said I'm not taking you to meet the hockey players unless you stop cutting class. Play games after school, or not at all. Do something outside. And I'll be checking on you, okay?"

He held up both his hands. "Okay, okay, I won't cut anymore. But you call me as soon as you talk to the guy about when we can go. And ask him if I can bring Jake, okay?"

Before she could answer, her phone buzzed in her pocket. "Oh, it's probably your mom calling me back," she said as she fished it out. "Maybe we can hit the movies tonight after all." But her stomach dropped a bit when she saw the caller ID. "It's work," she said, putting it to her ear.

"Claire, you better get back," Colby said, his voice all-business.

"Why, what's going on?"

"The captain called. Bart was found unconscious and Vince is gone." He hesitated.

"What?" Claire's stomach lurched. "What else?"

"Rafe's gone as well. He said he'd be right back, but he's not in the building."

Claire could hear the edge of tension in Colby's voice as he continued. "He walked out a few minutes after you. I thought he was going to get a drink or something."

Tightening her grip on the phone, Claire took a deep breath. "You don't have any idea where either of them are?"

"No. I'm headed back to the Axis office."

Claire clenched her jaw. "I'm on my way," she said, before closing her phone. She looked down at Will. "I have to go into work."

"I heard," he said, and his voice was back to having an angry edge.

"Hey," she said, lightly elbowing him. "We still have the hockey game to look forward to. And I will be checking in."

He ducked his head. "All right. But don't forget to see if Jake can come."

She smiled. "I will. Stay in class, little brother. Don't forget. And I'll call you. Soon."

He took a deep breath. "Okay." He didn't sound convinced of her sincerity and Claire's heart hurt.

"I promise I'll be a better sister, Will." She turned and gave him a stiff hug, his arms remaining at his side, his teenage body lankier and more solid than she remembered.

After about second or two, he softened, encircled her waist, and squeezed. "Thanks, Claire."

"I love you, Will," she said into his ear. "And Dad loves you, too. You have a lot of people who care about you."

He didn't say anything, just gripped her harder for a moment before letting go. "You better get back."

They walked to the front so Claire could pay and Will could get his pie, then headed back to visitor parking. Claire watched as he got into his car. "Drive carefully," she instructed. He gave her a smile before he shut his door and started the car.

She waved as he pulled out of the lot. It wasn't too late. She could still make this up to Will and be the sister she should have been. Like the brother Luke had always been to her.

But now it was time to get down to business.

Chapter Seven

Rafe's reflexes took over. *Deflect the weapon, destroy the grip, disarm.* When he had possession of the gun, he elbowed the gunman in the solar plexus. The guy was toned, but Rafe heard him suck in air when his elbow connected. Stepping forward, he clenched the gun in his hand, pointing it at the man who was now bent over and cradling his wrist. "Who are you?" Rafe demanded.

The man laughed as he straightened. "Don't you recognize me?"

Rafe felt like he'd been ambushed as he stared at the man's face. It was a little thinner and his beard was a bit thicker, but he would recognize him anywhere. "Bez Ruhallah." It was all Rafe could do not to let his mouth gape open in surprise.

"You remember me then." Bez took a step forward, stopping only when Rafe's finger twitched on the trigger. "It was so dark the night of my capture, I wasn't sure you would."

It wouldn't have mattered if Rafe had seen his face that night. He'd been staring at surveillance photos of Bez Ruhallah for more than a month before they'd grabbed him. As Osama bin Laden's driver, he'd been a high value target. "How did you get into this country?" The last time Rafe had seen Bez, he'd been on the border of Pakistan, being flown away on a Chinook helicopter under guard.

"Your government questioned me for a month at a detention facility before I went to Guantanamo. I spent eight months there until they decided I was reformed and had no other information to give them." He scowled. "You can't imagine what being in that prison was like." He hissed out a long bitter breath as if he'd been holding it in since his detainment started.

"They wouldn't have let you go. Not with what we had on you."

At that, Bez smiled. "Your government provided a lawyer that helped them see I was only a lowly driver and didn't know anything. And then, when they felt sorry enough for me, I got a free ride home. Fools."

"What do you want here?"

"At first, I wanted what was stolen from the amir. But then, when I realized you were connected to Axis, I wanted revenge for everything I have suffered." He pounded his chest with his fist. "I want you to endure what I have." He inched forward, his eyes on Rafe. "I want the amir's file so I can rebuild his empire and put America in her place, but if I can destroy it so that no one has it, that will work, too."

"By amir, I'm guessing you're referring to your boss, Osama bin Laden, since you pledged your life to him." Rafe let out a disgusted snort. "They should have let you rot in that prison." He clenched his fist, fuming inside. All of the intel they'd received had said Bez Ruhallah had earned his nickname of Bez the Butcher. He'd been an assassin for Osama and knew the intricacy of the al-Qaeda network almost as well as bin Laden had. How had he been allowed freedom?

He stretched his arm out further, the gun in his hand heavy. He had an al-Qaeda operative standing in front of him. One who wanted to destroy him and America. No one would blame Rafe if he killed him right now. Bez had killed hundreds of people in bombings and assassinations around the world. And he'd killed Gary. Rafe could end it all. "I want you to kneel down." He pointed the gun at Bez's heart. "Now."

Bez complied, putting his hands on top of his head. "Are you going to shoot an unarmed man, just as your government did when they murdered the amir?"

"Stop calling him that. Osama bin Laden wasn't a general or a prince. He was a terrorist." Rafe stepped closer until he was standing over Bez, touching the gun to the top of his head. "Just. Like. You."

His voice sounded far away when he spoke. Bez was so still. Rafe could hear his own heartbeat ramping up as the adrenaline flowed through him. He looked down at Bez, kneeling, and knew in that moment he couldn't do it. It would be cold-blooded murder. But he could put him back in a detention facility where he belonged and this time Rafe would make sure he stayed there. For Gary.

"Get up." Rafe stepped back so Bez could stand. Dropping the gun to his side, he turned slightly and in that split second Bez kicked out, slamming him in the thigh right above his injured knee. Barely biting back the cry of pain that rose to his lips, Rafe collapsed to the floor, unable to do more than grip his leg.

Bez quickly took back the gun. "Americans always want to be honorable. It's a weakness."

"I don't expect you to understand honor. But you do have a boatload of trouble about to come down on your head," Rafe gritted out, now looking down the barrel of the gun.

Bez stood over him, nudging his toe against Rafe's back. "Do you think I haven't prepared well for this day?" He leaned down. "Although I wasn't expecting to have such a hard time finding the amir's file. I have searched and it isn't in the main computer, but I know Mr. Holman had the encryption key and I want it. You're going to bring it to me."

"I don't think so." Rafe sat up, keeping a firm grip on his leg and his eyes on Bez.

"I think so." His voice mockingly imitated Rafe. Bez took a step back, but kept the gun firmly trained on Rafe's chest. "If you want to see your brother alive again, you're going to bring me what I want. You have three days to meet me at the Intercontinental Hotel in Kabul. I'm sure you remember it from your time in Afghanistan. I have to see you've brought the file and the key to it—" he paused to nod down at Rafe—"and I know enough about the amir's plans to know whether you've brought me the true file or not. Once you've brought it to me and I've authenticated it, I'll tell you where you can find your brother."

Rafe's insides twisted. "And if I don't?"

"Then I will send your brother back, piece by piece. I don't think you would like that, no?"

Bez walked toward the door and Rafe knelt on his good knee. *Can I stand?* He was going to try. With a little maneuvering and his teeth clenched so hard he wondered if they would crack under the pressure, he stood. Rafe took a tiny step forward, unsure of how much more his knee could take if he went hand-to-hand with Bez. If it came down to that, though, he would fight for his country. Or his life. "You're not going to have a chance to hurt my brother. There's no way you're getting out of here. This place is crawling with cops and Homeland Security."

"You underestimate me and my hatred for you and everything about your country." He stopped, pointing down at his clothing. "I'm dressed like everyone else searching this building. I even have a nametag." He flipped it up against his chest for emphasis. "But just to make sure I have time to leave without any detection, I've planted explosives. Once I leave, you've got six minutes to get that key, wherever Gary's hidden it, and clear the floor. Innocent people will die." Bez chuckled, the sound grating on Rafe's ears. "Not that there are any *innocents* in this country. Of course, if you are killed and the file is destroyed along with you, then, no matter, your brother will still die."

Rafe took two steps toward Bez, grateful he could put weight on his knee, but hoping he could keep Bez talking while he got a bit closer. "I don't know where the file or the key is! You can't sentence my brother to die because Gary didn't share his hiding place with anyone."

Bez shook his head. "There is no doubt in my mind you know where that file is and you will bring it to me to save your brother. But maybe I have over-estimated you. No matter. Either I will have that key, or no one will. You have six minutes."

Rafe held out a hand, trying to keep his voice calm. "You don't need to do that. I'll do what you ask. You don't have to set off any bombs."

"That's close enough." Bez put his hand on the door handle. "I know you want to kill me. I see that in your face. But this six minutes is my insurance policy that you'll do exactly as I say. Will you find the key and save your brother or warn the officers and try to save them? I don't think you can do both." He gave Rafe a mock salute, a tiny remote button visible in his palm. "I'll see you in Kabul in 72 hours. Your six minutes start right now." And with that, he twisted the handle and walked into the hall, disappearing quickly. The door slammed behind him.

Yanking it open again, Rafe followed him partway down the hall, but he couldn't keep up. And if Bez was telling the truth, Rafe had to get to that server room. Fast. Rafe half-ran with a limp in his gait to get back to Vince's desk, grab his keycard and get down the hall and around the corner to the server room. Gary had shown him his little spot just two weeks ago. If the file wasn't there . . . Rafe couldn't think about that right now. It had to be there.

He heard the hum of the machines as he approached, but even once he was inside, besides that, the room was eerily quiet. And cold. Heading over to the far corner, Rafe saw the table Gary had set up, his monitor filled with sticky notes on the edges, and a little whiteboard to the side. Feeling behind the flat screen where Gary knew no one would look, Rafe quickly ripped off four small flash drives, all animal-shaped. Gary had told him it helped keep his work straight in his mind—he filed them by animal. Hastily pocketing a monkey, mole, dog, and an eagle flash drives, Rafe turned and headed back. He had to warn the officers. Thankfully the building had been evacuated of employees, or this could have been catastrophic.

A small moan stopped him in his tracks. Turning down a row of machines, Rafe saw Penny, bound and gagged, her eyes wide, tears ruining her makeup.

He instantly closed the distance between them, taking out her gag and working on the duct tape that bound her. It was tight, and Penny cried out as he worked, but he finally got it off. "Thank goodness you found me," she sobbed. "A man took Vince. I tried to stop them." Her voice rose to a wail. "I broke two nails trying to fight him off." She held up her hand to show him. With a sob, she buried her face in Rafe's chest and cried.

Rafe patted her back as he slipped an arm around her. "Penny, we've got to get out of here, now, or your nails won't be the only things broken." He stood, his arm supporting her as he helped her to stand with him. She grasped his hand in a death grip as they started for the door, but with her high heels, she couldn't keep up. Biting the inside of his cheek, he put her over his shoulder. "Sorry, but we're in a hurry."

His shoulder ached and his knee burned as he hurried to the hall. Knowing Bez hadn't given him quite enough time to grab the file and get everyone out made fury thrum through his veins. Bez was a sick and dangerous man—who had his brother and wanted him dead.

76

He exited the server room and just before Vince's office, two cops came from the opposite direction down the hall. "Hey," the older one called. "What's going on?"

"Do you have a radio? You need to evacuate this floor right now," Rafe yelled, inserting some authority into his voice. "There's a bomb set to go off any second. Get out!" He lurched toward the stairwell entrance, hoping to get somewhere safer than the point of impact. The officers didn't seem to question him as he heard them run down the hall, calling out bomb threat and evacuation codes on their radio. Rafe hoped he'd given them enough time. Meeting him on the stairs, one of the officers held out his arms for Penny. "Name's Joe. Let me help you."

Rafe handed her off to Joe, thinking he could get her down the stairs faster than if Rafe kept trying with an injured knee. Penny didn't seem to mind as Joe adjusted his stance so he could cradle her. She took one look at Joe and curled her arms around his neck. "Thank you for rescuing me," she said, her voice hitching on a sob. "You're a hero."

He started down the steps with a smile. "Yes, ma'am."

Rafe shook his head as they all descended, each of them trying to maneuver the stairs as fast as they could, Joe with Penny, his partner in the middle on the radio describing the situation, and Rafe trying to finesse his injured knee behind them. They just barely made it to the ground floor before they felt the building above them shake. "Get out!" Rafe shouted and they ran faster for the exit.

They shot out the back door, their heads down as glass and debris rained on them. Sprinting to the front, chaos was all around them as they emerged.

"I hope no one was hurt," Joe said as the three of them stopped in front of a knot of police cars. It didn't look like Penny was anxious for Joe to put her down. Rafe was glad she was okay. As other officers came toward them, he backed up and changed course for the parking garage. No one seemed to notice as he disappeared. Luckily he'd parked near the entrance and could see his car from the street. With one last glance around him, he unlocked his car. There wasn't any time to waste; he had a lot of arrangements to make if he was going to be in Kabul in 72 hours.

Sliding into the driver's seat, he thought how it seemed like forever ago he'd parked for his meeting with Vince. Letting out a breath, Rafe started the car and headed for the entrance. As he exited the garage, an officer appeared, holding up a hand to stop him, but Rafe waved him away. There just wasn't any more time to explain.

Rafe rolled down the windows, letting the cool air flow over him. Touching the outline of the flash drives in his pocket, he hoped he had the right ones. If he didn't, his brother's life would be worth nothing. *Maybe I can check out what I've got before I go.*

He raced toward home, going over in his mind the things he needed to pack and how he was going to get on a plane to Afghanistan. It didn't take long at the speed he was driving to make it up the hill to his parents' home, the large colonial alone at the top. Pulling through the gate he drove around the circular driveway to the garage. He pressed the garage button, waiting for it to fully open so he could pull the car in. With a last look at the trees that surrounded the house, he realized that while they offered privacy, they were also a security risk. The nearest neighbor was half a mile away, and they were surrounded by a little forest. Anyone could have been watching Vince, his parents—him. *Has Bez been here?*

He got out of the car, putting his hand in his pocket to reassure himself the flash drives were still there. They were all he had to bargain with. With a step forward, he made a mental note to take some pain meds with him. His body was begging for even a tiny relief from pain. As he inserted the key into the lock, the hairs on Rafe neck prickled. He took a look around, but not seeing anything, he turned the handle of the back door. That's when he heard a click—a small, tinny sound, one that a normal person probably wouldn't pay any attention to, but one that Rafe had been trained to listen for in his first year in the military. Knowing what that tiny click meant, he also knew he had mere seconds to get away. He ran, hoping his knee could hold him upright one more time as toe-curling pain shot up his leg.

Without a chance to even take another breath, Rafe's house exploded into a ball of flames behind him.

Chapter Eight

Claire's heart hammered against her chest as her car approached Rafe's home. Emergency vehicles were everywhere, the once manicured lawn obscured by them all parked haphazardly on it, and the acrid smell of smoke filled the air. She clenched her hands on the wheel, unable to look away from the burning home in front of her, but needing to keep her focus so she could zigzag around and find an open space to park. She resisted the urge to stop where she was, throw open the door, and run to the scene, but then her car would be blocking the way. *Did he survive the roof just to die at home?*

When she finally found an open square of lawn, she parked and slowly opened the door. Her chest tightened when she though about what condition she might find Rafe in. *How could this have happened?* she asked herself for the millionth time. Rubbing the middle of her forehead with two fingers, she closed her eyes and took a second to compose herself. When her professional face was securely in place, she stepped out of the car and started to the scene.

Flashing her badge through the crowd, she stood next to a firefighter who'd just come out of Rafe's home. He ran a hand over his brow, looking back at the flames shooting toward the night sky.

"That's going to be a total loss," he said, sadness in his voice. "Such a shame."

Claire shifted her stance a bit to lean closer to him so she could be heard over the shouts of the firemen and hissing flames. "Any news about the homeowner?"

"Last I heard the homeowners were in the hospital. One of them is recovering from a stroke. Their son is over in the ambulance." The man jerked his thumb to the left. "Some pretty bad burns, but from the sounds of it he'll live."

He left without a backward glance, not giving Claire time to ask him if he was sad about that, since he'd seemed more upset about the burning house than a burn victim. *He's doing his job. Cut him some slack.* She scraped the hair back from her face, letting it fall around her shoulders again. *At least Rafe was still alive.*

When she finally found him, he was on his stomach, the EMT treating a nasty burn over most of one shoulder blade. But it wasn't the burn that made Claire suck in a breath. Old scars covered almost every square inch of his upper back. It looked like the wounds had healed, but whatever had done that to him had to have been painful. The EMT finished and bandaged the burn that would join the rest of his scars.

"Hey," Claire said, quietly approaching them.

Rafe slowly turned his head to look at her, his cheeks smudged with soot. The scratch on his forehead looked like someone had run a nail over his face. "Hey," he said back. "Guess I should have waited for you."

Have they given him pain meds? He looks like he could use some. Claire didn't voice her thoughts. "Are you okay?"

He nodded. "I'll live."

"Barely, from the sounds of it. This wouldn't have happened if you'd stayed at the station and finished your statement with Colby. I don't like being lied to." The fear she'd had for him turned to anger.

"I didn't lie. I'd finished for the day and I left a number where I could be reached. I needed to get back to the office." He slowly raised to a sitting position. "They've got my brother."

Claire went very still. *Get more information before you react.* "What happened?"

"The man who killed Gary was in Vince's office when I got there. He gave me six minutes to grab a file and get everyone off the floor before it blew." He waved an arm back at the burning rubble that used to be his home. "I guess he thought he might make things harder for me if he blew up my house, too. Or maybe he just wants me dead."

Claire looked back at the house. "Yeah, the bombs at Axis only ended up being in three offices. Blew out a lot of windows, but it was more bang than anything. Thanks to your warning, no one was hurt. They're going to have to evaluate any structural damage before Axis is open for business again, though."

Rafe shook his head. "This is a personal vendetta because of a classified mission I was part of. Do we have someone guarding my parents?"

"I need more information before I can make that request." Claire rolled back on her heels.

He ran his hands through his hair. "I'm not in the mood to be debriefed or go through the third degree about something I can't talk about. Just believe me when I tell you . . . you know, never mind. I'll take care of it myself." He grabbed the white shirt hanging off the end of the gurney. "If you'll excuse me, I have somewhere to be." He started to walk away, but the EMT stopped him.

"Mr. Kelly, you need to go to the hospital and have that burn cleaned thoroughly. It could become infected if you don't, and believe me, you don't want that."

Rafe turned. "I'm fine. Just give me some ointment or whatever and I'll keep it clean."

"I'm not kidding. That burn needs care."

"If you need me to sign something I will, but I'm not going to the hospital."

Claire shook her head as the EMT retreated. "Since someone is trying to kill you, don't you think *you* need some protection? We could contain things at a hospital and you could get proper care."

"I don't want to go to the hospital."

"You just said someone wants you dead. It might be time to just lie low and think about your next move." Claire knew he would want to think strategically.

He closed his eyes. "I wouldn't be able to do that if I'm admitted to a hospital, but my parents are there. If it's easy to contain things, maybe you can take care of that and as soon as I know my parents are safe, I'll contact you with my whereabouts, okay? You don't have to worry about me."

"It's my job," Claire said evenly.

"I'm not a hostage, Claire." He turned to look down at her, his gaze smoldering with an emotion she couldn't identify. Anger? Frustration? Whatever it was, it gave her a tingle of warning.

She backed up a step. "No, but your brother is. Let me help you."

The EMT came toward them, a little baggie in his hand. "Here's some ointment and bandages. I strongly recommend you go to the hospital. Or at least follow up with your personal physician."

Rafe barely glanced at him. "Thanks." He took the baggie and turned to walk away.

"Rafe," she called, but he didn't answer her. She couldn't let it go. Hurrying after him, she matched his strides as he came to the edge of the driveway. "Where do you think you're going? You don't have a car, your house is pretty much ashes. You don't even have a shirt to wear." She gestured toward the shredded piece of fabric he'd thrown over his shoulders but been unable to button.

"Thanks for the damage report." He glared at her. "But really, why do you care? Isn't this above and beyond the call of duty? Or is there another reason?"

Claire bit her lip. "Yeah, I have my reasons."

"Like?" His tone was mocking as he raised his eyebrows. "The government's trained me to take care of myself. Or is that it? You have a thing for SEALs?"

He'd probably seen a lot of women fall over him with the combination of being a Navy SEAL and that little-boy vulnerability she'd glimpsed earlier today. *It certainly isn't because of his personality.* He obviously wouldn't recognize a sincere offer to help if it bit him. "You know what? You don't want my help, fine. Take care of it yourself and good luck with that." She walked away, feeling proud of herself for carefully controlling her tone when she'd wanted to slap that arrogant look off his face. She dug what little nails she had into the palm of her hand. *What was I thinking trying to help him?*

Crossing the last bit of lawn before her car, she was approached by two men in suits. The taller one quickly flashed a badge at her. "Are you Detective Michaels?"

"Yes." She stepped around them toward her car. "I'm in a hurry." The man blocked her way and she gave him her frostiest look.

"I'm afraid we haven't been properly introduced. I'm Ryan Johnson and this is my partner Greg Farley. Homeland Security. Since we didn't get to talk this afternoon, we need to speak this evening."

Claire held in an exasperated breath. "I'm right in the middle of an investigation. Maybe I can take your card . . ." She stepped around them again and made it to the driver's side.

"Unfortunately, while you *were* the lead investigator on record, this is just a courtesy to tell you that Homeland has jurisdiction over this case. Since things have now escalated, we're going to need to put Mr. Kelly under our protection." He pointed back at the house.

Claire stared at them and clenched her jaw. *Courtesy?* "I'm going to have to talk to my captain about this."

"That's fine," Agent Johnson said. "Let us know if you have any questions, but in the meantime, could you tell us where Mr. Kelly is?"

Hopefully drowning in the lake I saw as I pulled into the driveway. "I'm looking for him myself," she said smoothly. *Let them do their own work on the case, including finding Rafe.* She looked Agent Farley in the eye, making her voice as strong and confident as she could. "I think someone said he was getting his burns treated."

"We're going to need your file on this," he continued. "But we'll be sitting down with you and your captain in the morning." He handed her his card before he walked toward the house.

Claire watched them go, biting the inside of her cheek. She had nothing against Homeland; she'd worked with them before. But she wanted this case. No matter what was going on with Rafe Kelly, she could still investigate Gary's death.

Just as she was about to get into her car, Rafe approached out of the darkness. "Can I talk to you?"

"About what?" She leaned on the car door, tilting her head toward him. "I think you said it all back there. Or did you come back to see if I was pining for you?"

He shoved his hands in his pants pockets. "I'm sorry."

"Rafe, I was offering my help because of my experience both as a detective and a hostage negotiator. That's all. Whether you believe me or not." Claire took a step backward.

"I know." He moved quickly toward her and took hold of the top of the door as if he thought she were going to leave. "I actually could use some help, if you're still willing."

"You don't need me. Homeland Security was just here, looking for you. I'm sure they'd be willing to help."

"They're just the people I don't need. I've got to get out of here. Vince's life depends on it."

Claire bit her lip. *Don't get involved. It's too close to home. Too close to what happened to my own brother.* "What do you need?" she finally said, overriding her brain's objections.

"Your car." He looked over at the dying orange glow from the house. "I promise to let you know where I leave it."

"You want me to just give you my car. Without any questions?" Claire was incredulous. *This guy is unbelievable.* Keeping her tone professional, she countered. "In the twelve hours or so since I've known you, you've almost been killed three times. I think you need backup. And I'm not giving you my car."

Rafe immediately shook his head. "Listen, I appreciate all you've done for me, but I can't risk your life again by involving you in this." He motioned toward the bandage on her neck.

She grabbed at her duty belt, pulling her badge toward the light. "This shiny little shield here isn't a prize I got out of a candy box. I'm a detective. I'm *already* involved." She leaned forward, lowering her voice. "I was there on that roof today, too, Rafe."

"You were shot today, too." Rafe tried to take a step and stumbled, catching himself on the hood. Cursing, he straightened slowly, his back obviously causing him pain.

"Well, I'm still standing which is more than I can say for you." She reached for his hand, hoping to steady him, but he drew it back.

"I've seen your negotiating skills, which were pretty good," he admitted. "But how well do you handle a gun?" He tilted his head, giving her a don't-lie-to-me look.

"You don't have to insult me. I've been going to firing ranges since I was a teenager."

Rafe raised his eyebrow.

"My dad was in the military."

She could see the Homeland agents drawing near the driveway again. Claire held her breath. The invisible cord pulling her to this case could be broken right here. "Rafe, either you take my help or Homeland Security is going to put you under their protection. You decide."

Rafe narrowed his eyes, then held out his hand as if he were making a silent agreement with her.

"Good choice." She shook it. Hard.

He walked around the door and slid slowly into the driver's seat, what was left of the shirt fabric not doing much to cover his back or his burn.

Claire stood next to the open driver's side door, looking down at him. "I think I should drive, since it's my car and I know where we're going."

"I think you should let *me* drive, since I know where I'm taking you."

"I can take you to a safe house with a secure line where you can get some clothes. Definitely a place you can strategize your next move and have privacy." She folded her arms and leaned her hip against the frame. "Can you top that?"

He propped his arms on steering wheel, looking up at her. "Well, if you'd said you had a holocaust cloak and a wheelbarrow among your assets I would have been more impressed."

She couldn't help herself. She laughed. "Very funny. I could probably get you the wheelbarrow for sure. The holocaust cloak is iffy." She shot him a curious glance. "I'm surprised you know that movie."

"*Princess Bride?* It's a classic. Is there anyone who doesn't know it?"

"Sorry, you don't seem like the type of guy that could relax and enjoy the *Princess Bride*."

"Well, you shouldn't judge people." He stepped out of the car, motioning for her to get in. "Do you really have all that?"

She gave him her best are-you-kidding-me look. "Did you think I was just trying to impress you?"

"Maybe."

So infuriating. "Now who's judging?" She brushed by him and got into the vacated driver's seat. "Don't worry, I have no problem putting my money where my mouth is." When he was next to her in the passenger seat, she started the car, going back down to the main road.

"Where is this haven of privacy and security that no one else can top?" He shifted in his seat, working to find a comfortable position.

"It's my father's house." She swallowed. "He's rarely there. And you could borrow some of my brother's clothes. I think you're about the same height and build." She tried to keep the tremor out of her voice, but couldn't.

Rafe was quiet for a moment. "Your brother won't mind?"

"No." It took all of her resolve, but she was proud of herself for sounding so normal. Sometimes the grief still overwhelmed her and she didn't want Rafe to witness that.

Out of the corner of her eye she could see Rafe gingerly run his hand through his hair and scrunch up his face. *What is he doing?*

"I don't know. Your place? This is all happening so fast. I need time to think."

His expression was so comical as he over-acted the innocent look, she could hardly choke back another laugh. *Infuriating and funny.* "You're safe with me," Claire assured him with a grin, glad for a change of subject.

He chuckled. "You know, you're beautiful when you smile. You should try it more often."

"You're so bossy." She mimicked his voice. "Give me your

89

car, don't judge, smile more."

This time he laughed and held up his hands in surrender. "Okay, okay, I'll try to do better in the bossiness department."

"Thank you." Claire leaned back in her seat, her spirits lifted. After the day they'd had, it did feel good to relax for a second. But as soon as her mind went there, she knew she had to get serious. There were decisions to be made, lives on the line. *Should I call my dad about this?* He might be able to help. Glancing at Rafe, she decided to wait. One step at a time.

"Hang on," she said as she pressed down on the accelerator.

Chapter Nine

Rafe looked over at Claire as they sped through city streets, trying to keep the concern from his face. She'd looked so sad, he was glad he'd made her laugh. She obviously needed more laughter in her life. He shifted his gaze to stare at the oncoming traffic, remembering how her face had lit up when she'd smiled at him. She was beautiful, but more than that, she was good at her job and cared about helping others. He wished he hadn't run his mouth about her motives. The fact was, he was worried about involving anyone else in this. It was going to get dangerous and he didn't want her hurt. With the way things were right now, though, he needed her. *I'll protect her,* he vowed.

"How much longer until we get there?" he asked, wanting to fill the silence.

"About twenty minutes." Claire moved restlessly in her seat. Something was bothering her, but he couldn't put his finger on it. "Are you sure this is going to be okay?"

She nodded. "Trust me, I've got you covered."

He thought of how calm she'd been on the roof, how she'd still wanted to work the case after being shot. And how concerned she'd been about him. "Thanks, Claire."

Claire glanced at him and narrowed her eyes, as if she were trying to read his thoughts. "You're welcome, but it's all about saving my honor now and proving to you I keep my promises."

"You don't have to prove anything to me."

"I know, but I will just this once." She drove down a block of townhouses then parked. Getting out, she led him to a unit in the middle of the block. Claire took him around back, going at his pace up the small steps. Pulling out her key, she put it in the lock and released a deep breath before turning it.

She walked in, the moonlight giving off just enough light for Rafe to make out the small dining area to her right and the hall that led to the front of the house. Claire didn't turn on a light though. She seemed frozen to the spot, and when Rafe looked closer, he could see that her eyes were closed.

"Claire, is everything okay?" Rafe came up behind her, as close as he dared. *Had she lost too much blood earlier? Was she going to faint?* He got in a position to catch her, just in case.

But she didn't faint. She moved forward. "I'm fine." She flicked on the lights. "There's a dining room and kitchen over here," she pointed, "and the office and living room is this way." She walked down the hall, her shoes quiet on the hardwood floor.

She paused in the office doorway and Rafe heard her take one more deep breath before stepping in. He followed, curious as to why she was being affected this way. It looked like every other office he'd ever been in. A desk. A library of books. A window seat.

"It's just the same," Claire whispered. Rafe was barely able to hear her.

"You haven't been here in a while?"

"No." She walked over to the window seat, her voice sounding distant. "The last time I was here, we were all waiting for word."

Rafe leaned against the doorway, careful of his shoulder. "Waiting for word of what?"

Claire avoided his eyes and motioned toward the couch on the other side of the desk. "Why don't you make yourself comfortable? I'll go get some clothes for you."

He caught her arm before she could go through the doorway. "Waiting for word of what?" he repeated softly.

"Waiting to see if my brother was dead or alive. That's why I wanted to help you save your brother." Her voice was strangled, as if there was a lump in her throat she couldn't speak through.

His entire body tensed at her words and he didn't know what to say. It hit him how big of a jerk he'd been earlier. *She wants to help me save my brother because she's been where I am.* "I'm really sorry, Claire." He touched her shoulder and she leaned into him for a moment. Encouraged, he reached an arm behind her back, drawing her closer to his side.

Claire pulled away and ran her hand over her eyes. "Sorry," she murmured. "I haven't been here in a long time and it brought back a lot of memories."

He moved, turning the side-hug into a full-on hug, feeling her tremble in his arms. She didn't move and he thought about releasing her, but she slowly drew her arms up to encircle his waist. They stayed like that, drawing and giving comfort. Rafe couldn't remember a time when he'd ever felt such an understanding with another human being. Loath to break the moment, he hesitated, but needed an answer. "Are you sure you're okay?"

She didn't say anything at first, just drew back slightly to look at him. "We'll get your brother back," she told him, all trace of trembling gone. "I'll do everything I can. I promise."

He brushed her hair from her face, his thumb trailing over her cheekbone and down to her neck where the white bandage lay as a testament to her commitment of protecting others. "I know you will," he said. "You have no idea how grateful I am for that right now. I really am sorry."

She raised her chin and licked her lips. For just an instant Rafe wanted to kiss her, but she stepped away and the moment was gone. "I'll go get you those clothes."

It was obvious she'd needed a moment alone. The truth was, Rafe did, too. *What am I doing?* As soon as she left the room, Rafe shoved a hand through his hair, the worry over Vince slamming back into him. He walked to the desk, lifting a picture so he could sit on the edge. Three people smiled into the camera—Claire in the middle of two men, both in uniform, both looking remarkably like her.

Feeling a little like he'd invaded her privacy, he put the picture back, moved to the couch and sat down, being careful of his injuries. Within moments Claire was back in the room, holding a pair of sweats, a t-shirt, and an ice pack. "Thought your knee might need a little care," she said.

"Thanks." *That's thoughtful.* He took the clothes, searching her face for any sign of tears.

"There's a bathroom just through there." She pointed to a little door in the corner of the room. "While you change, I'll get us something to eat. Then we can work on what we're going to do next."

She was back to all-business. *Well, I prefer this Claire anyway,* he decided. He nodded and stood, watching her. When he didn't move, she raised her chin, and in that moment he saw how vulnerable she was in this room. The memories weren't good ones and it was easy to see how hard this was for her. "Maybe we should go somewhere else, Claire."

She lowered her eyes and when she looked back up at him, they were guarded, her defenses back up and in position. "I think we better stick with the plan. It's the best one we've got."

With raised eyebrows and a shrug, he headed for the bathroom. He'd let it ride for now. If she thought she could handle it, who was he to question it? Closing the bathroom door behind him, he tried to block out the memory of Claire's sadness and how curious he was about her and her family.

When he had washed up as best he could and changed into the sweats and t-shirt, the flash drives safe in the sweatpants' pocket, he opened the door to Claire setting down a plate of sandwiches and an aromatic steaming mug of hot chocolate, if he wasn't mistaken. He walked toward her, a smile on his face. "Do you know how long it's been since I had hot chocolate?"

He sat with one leg on the cushion so he could adjust the cold pack for his knee. Claire barely looked at him, her focus on the paper in front of her. "I jotted down a few questions while you were changing."

Rafe raised his eyebrows, looking at about half a page of writing. "A few?"

She read off the first three. "What kind of mission in Afghanistan gets personal on U.S. soil? What file does Axis have that is so valuable? Why are the CIA and Homeland Security involved?"

Rafe settled back against the couch. "Good questions."

Claire pulled out her phone. "Well, maybe I can answer one of them. My dad's been calling me since you were on the roof today. Maybe he knows something."

"Why would your father know anything about this?"

Hesitating, Claire stared at her phone.

"Claire?"

"My dad is the Chief of the National Clandestine Service."

"Your dad is Skip Michaels?" Rafe's tone was incredulous.

"You know him?"

"Well, I know *of* him. My last assignment was with the Special Activities Division."

"How can that be? They usually only take former SEALs, not active-duty ones."

"We knew the area from a former mission and it was remote enough that they needed us." Rafe ran his hand over his chin. "I can't believe Skip Michaels is your father. Everyone knows him. He had some amazing experiences when he was a Marine. Not to mention when he was over in Africa as the Deputy Chief."

"Yeah, I've heard all about the legend."

Rafe put down his sandwich. "And that means your brother was Luke Michaels."

"You've heard of him?"

Her voice was wary and Rafe wondered if he should take the conversation any further. "Is there anyone who doesn't remember when he was taken hostage in Iraq?" He kept his comments careful and as neutral as he could.

"No, I guess not." She raised her chin to look him squarely in the face.

His stomach sank, remembering the grainy images of Luke, blindfolded, kneeling down in front of the TV camera as he stated his name and rank. He couldn't imagine what Claire had been through. After nine days, the U.S. had mounted a rescue mission, but Luke had been killed during the firefight. The entire nation had grieved over his loss. "I'm sorry, Claire. I don't know what to say. I wish there was something I could do."

She gave him a tight smile, then pressed the phone to her ear. There wasn't anything he could do and he knew it as well as anyone. "Dad?" she said into her phone. "I got a message that you've been trying to reach me." She paused, listening. "Yes, I saw the bomb." She glanced over at Rafe. "I know where Rafe Kelly is. Sitting right here on your couch."

Rafe realized he was bouncing his knee and forced himself to stop. *Is this a secure line?* Of course it was. Her dad was part of the

CIA. It was hard to wrap his brain around the fact that her dad was Skip Michaels.

"We're in your office. I hope you don't mind." From the way she grimaced, it was apparent he *did* mind. "Plan B? Are you sure that's needed?"

"What's Plan B?" Rafe mouthed to her.

She glanced away, suddenly standing. "Dad, I don't think that's necessary." Walking to the window, she peeked out. "Okay. Plan B. I'll do the check-in tomorrow." Snapping the phone shut, she took three long strides to Rafe's side. "Come on, we've got to get out of here." She held out her hand.

"Get out of here? Why?"

"You're in trouble. We've got to go to Plan B." She grabbed his arm and tried to haul him up. "A lot of people are looking for you."

Rafe stood. "Did your father say much else?"

"He's going to check in with us tomorrow. Until then, I've got to keep you under wraps. The U.S. government wants to speak with you pretty badly. Seems there's been some blowback from Operation Eagle Claw."

Rafe ran his hand over his face, surprised to hear that come out of her mouth. "What did he tell you about that? That's classified."

"Nothing except that, so don't worry. Your secrets are safe. But we've got to get out of here. My dad doesn't activate Plan B for fun." She was already gathering up his ice pack.

"What is Plan B exactly?" Rafe reached back for his shredded shirt and suit pants and grabbed one more sandwich.

"You'll see," Claire said grimly as she walked through the door. It was obvious she expected him to follow.

"I don't like the sound of that." He caught her at the back door where they'd come in.

She put her finger to her lips, peeking through the curtain that covered the door window. "Get ready."

Rafe shoved the rest of his sandwich into his mouth and nodded. She held up her fingers, counting down, 3,2,1.

Then she opened the door.

Chapter Ten

Claire kept her back against the wall, the bricks digging into her back. She could hear heavy footsteps coming down the front walk and she waited until they climbed the stairs. When she heard the doorbell ring, she ran across the yard. As she lifted an arm to go over the fence, her chest twinged, the pain telling her this wasn't going to be easy. Quickly sticking a toe into the chain link she hauled herself over.

Thankfully Rafe was right behind her doing the same thing. She dropped behind a large landscaping bush and felt Rafe's hand on her back. "We need to get to the car," she whispered just as Agent Farley came into view.

She could feel Rafe's hand tense and they both crouched there, stock-still. They watched him sweep the yard, coming within feet of them, but moving on. "Clear," he called to his partner still in the front.

When he left, they both moved as quickly as possible across two more yards, and Claire was grateful they both had short fences. Flattening themselves against the corner of the brownstone down the street from her father's, Claire could see her car. "I'm going to peek around the corner and see where the agents are." Rafe nodded. When she didn't see them, she knew they had probably gone back to their own car to wait. This was going to be risky if they were watching the street carefully.

"Let's go separately, and keep in between the other cars as much as possible."

"Maybe I should go first. Just in case."

"No. Just follow my lead." Claire didn't wait to argue with Rafe further, instead she started down the line of cars. When she was two away from her car, she darted across the street and around the car. With measured movements, she opened the passenger side and climbed in, leaving it open for Rafe. She couldn't see him and hoped he hadn't decided to run. *Maybe I should have let him go first.*

Claire gasped when he pulled the door open wider. She hadn't even heard him coming. "Covert ops taught me a thing or two," he said with a satisfied smile, knowing he'd startled her.

"Stay down," she instructed, finding it hard to suppress a smile of her own at his boldness. She pulled the car out of its space and headed for the safe house, glancing in the rearview mirror to make sure they weren't being followed. That had been close. How had they found her so quickly? Homeland research department must be getting better.

Her stomach was still in knots from the close getaway and the fact that evading Homeland Security was serious. It made her apprehensive, even if her father thought it was necessary. From what he said on the phone, several agencies were looking for Rafe, but it was important that the NCS talk to him first. So he'd called a Plan B and it was up to her to carry it out.

She headed for the safe house, acutely aware that Rafe was staring at her. "What?" she finally asked.

"Where are we going?"

"Somewhere safe."

"You said the last place was safe."

"Okay, somewhere *safer*. If you're as exhausted as I am, we're going to need a place to rest. My dad will brief us tomorrow on the situation."

"What did he say, exactly?"

"Like I told you, the government wants to talk to you. My dad wants to be first in line."

Rafe folded his arms and looked out the window. With barely any traffic on the road and the moonlight being so thin, Claire couldn't see his expression well enough to read it.

"What are you thinking about?" She finally asked, the curiosity getting the best of her. She put the car into park, the silhouette of the Keney Clock Tower looming in front of them.

"What, no offer of even a penny for my thoughts?" He gave her a wry smile. "To tell the truth I'm hoping my brother is still alive and will stay that way until I can get to him. Bez gave me a pretty strict timetable and I don't have time to play cat and mouse right now." He ran his hands through his hair before stopping to rub his neck.

"We'll get him back, Rafe." She put all the optimism into her voice that she could.

"No one can be sure about that. Look at how it turned out for your brother."

There had been an unspoken comfortableness between them since her dad's house, but that evaporated with his words. Hurt and anger rose in her, her emotions too close to the surface. *Why did I confide in him about Luke?* She turned away to open the car door, but he reached over and grabbed her arm. "I'm sorry, Claire. I didn't mean that."

Another car's headlights illuminated the car for a moment and Claire looked at him sitting there, his eyes staring at her bandaged neck. She'd caught him looking at it several times today, and every time he did, it seemed to make him feel guilty. It was starting to bother her. But, he'd suffered with the death of his friend and not knowing what happened to his brother. She'd been where he was with his brother and could cut him a little slack. "I think we both need to get some rest."

"Is this where we're staying tonight?" He waved toward the tower.

Claire nodded. "Sort of. I was just running my protocols. Making sure we're not followed." She started the car again, going around the side of the tower toward a small church. "We've got a little room here at the church with a go bag. We should be safe tonight."

Claire kept her eyes open, all of her senses on alert. She didn't feel like there was any danger lurking, but she wanted to be careful. With one more turn around the property, she parked the car near a little shed where it couldn't be seen without effort. They got out and walked to the back of the church, up the old stone steps. Claire picked up one of the bare flowerpots at the back door, producing a key. Unlocking the door, she led them through a short hallway and opened the door at the end of the hall. It was an office with a cot and recliner near the back.

"How come you have a key to a church?" he asked her.

Claire smiled. "It's a long story and it's late." She pointed down the hall. "The only other rooms here are the chapel, a bathroom, and a little storage room. But we'll be safe."

Rafe looked at the tiny cot, then back at her. "We should probably take turns on watch. Do you want first or second?"

He looked down at her, and Claire could see how tired he was. "Why don't you get some sleep first," she told him. "I'm good."

"You're a terrible liar," he said, pushing her into the room. "I'll come wake you in a few hours."

Not wanting to be alone just yet, she turned to face him, holding the door open. "You know, I think we're safe here. That's why it's always our Plan B. If you want, you could lie down on one of the pews in the chapel. It'd be long enough for you. Not exactly comfortable, and only marginally better than a hard floor, but you wouldn't be fighting to keep yourself awake." She brushed by and headed for the larger room, not waiting for his reply in case he was going to argue with her again.

Rafe followed, looking around at the little chapel. Stained glass windows surrounded them and the pews on either side looked like they'd been there for a hundred years.

"How old is this place?"

"I don't know. Pretty old." She moved up the aisle, stopping a few feet in front of him. She let her fingers glide over the polished wood. This wood had probably been witness to many a whispered confession, she thought. Looking back at Rafe, she bit the inside of her lip. "So, what do you think?"

He looked down at the length of the pew. "It might work. My feet wouldn't hang over the edge or anything. And it's a perfect Plan B. I mean, who would attack us in a church, right?" He chuckled as she drew near. "I think I'll sleep near the back, though, just in case I need a quick exit."

She stopped directly in front of him, feeling a tightening in her chest as she thought of what they'd been through today. "You must have known very little peace in Afghanistan," she said softly. "And then to come home to this . . ." Her voice trailed off. She stared at him, wishing she could read him better. He seemed to be so in control of his expressions and emotions when she wanted to know his thoughts.

"Does any soldier feel peace, really, no matter where they are?"

"I'd like to think they can." *I want to think Luke did, even at the end.*

"Probably about as much as you do in your job." Rafe reached for her, resting his hand on her shoulder. "Is that why you became a hostage negotiator? Because of what happened to your brother?"

His face was shadowed in the darkness, making the moment intimate and anonymous. Regardless of her mind warning her to be careful, she instinctively knew she trusted him with her secrets. "Yes. I never wanted to feel that helpless again." There. She'd said it out loud to another human being. She stepped closer, wanting to feel the warmth and comfort he'd offered her earlier. Boldly, she put her hands on his chest, letting them slide up to his shoulders.

He bent his head, his voice low in her ear. "I can't imagine you helpless."

She looked up at him, standing on her tiptoes. Their eyes locked as Claire ran a hand from his temple to his jaw. She let her thumb trace his bottom lip, her heart starting to race. "That's because I'm not." And then she lightly pressed her lips to his.

The spark between them flared to life as he instantly pulled her tight in his arms. His lips were soft and sure, exploring hers with an intensity she'd never felt before. Rafe's touch made her shiver against him as he ran his hands up her back, stopping to cup her face. With a groan he tangled his hands in her hair, gently tugging until she lifted her chin and exposed her neck. He trailed a line of kisses from her cheek to her ear and she hung onto his shoulders, knowing that was the only thing holding her upright. Opening her eyes, she took his face in her hands and brought her lips back to his. The kiss deepened and Claire knew she was treading dangerous ground with this man, this stranger, feeling a sense of wholeness that she didn't think she ever would feel with someone.

She drew her head back until their foreheads touched, her breath mingling with his as she tried to slow it down. "I'm sorry," she whispered.

He let her step away from him, but kept hold of her left hand, holding it over his heart. "I'm not." She could feel his sprinting heartbeat underneath her fingers and was glad the kiss had affected him as well. "Claire, I have to tell you something."

Cold reality washed over her and she steeled herself. *Will he reject me outright? Accuse me of only kissing him because he's a SEAL?* "What?"

"I know the man who took Vince. His full name is Bez Ruhallah. He was a high value target, but he was released. He's after the encryption key that Gary talked about on the roof. Sort of. He did say if he couldn't have it, he just didn't want the U.S. to have it." He ran a lock of her hair through her fingers, making the butterflies in her stomach start up again, before he tucked it behind her ear. "If I get it, he instructed me to meet him in Kabul in three days or he's going to start sending Vince home in pieces."

Claire chewed on her bottom lip. This was big. Not only the information, but the fact he was trusting her with it. "Do you have the key to trade for Vince?" Rafe nodded. "Do you know what's on the file being decrypted?"

"No. But Gary died for it and Vince might, too. I'd sure like to know how Bez found out Gary had it."

Claire cracked her thumb knuckles. She'd always meant to break that habit, but never seemed to get around to it. "There's a computer in the office. Maybe we can take a look at what's so important."

"Are you sure? There might not be any turning back once we look at this." His voice had a thread of concern. "So far, the people who have seen it are dead or missing."

"I'm in." Claire gave him a small smile, knowing the time for turning back had passed long ago. She took his hand. "Let's go."

He led her back to the office, but once there, she quickly dropped his hand and went to the desk to turn on the computer. "Is it on a flash drive?"

Rafe nodded. "Actually, there are four of them. I didn't know which one I needed so I took them all." He handed her four little flash drives shaped like animals.

Claire chuckled. "Why animals?"

"He said that's how he filed them in his mind." Rafe laughed with her. "I can only imagine what's on the mole and monkey files. I'm guessing the one we want is the eagle."

She plugged that one in first. Coming around the desk, Rafe stared at the screen over her shoulder. At first, it looked like circling letters. Gibberish. But as it swirled around the screen, suddenly it went blank, asking for a password and a fingerprint. Presumably Gary's.

"Try Eagle Claw for the password."

Claire typed it in. Nothing. "Nope. And it looks like we need both the fingerprint and the password. Any other ideas?"

"No." Rafe ran his fingers through his hair. "If Gary was the only one with the encryption key, Vince is in a lot of trouble."

"Let's try the other three." Claire plugged them all in, but they all were full of gibberish that needed a password and a fingerprint. "We definitely need that key to decrypt the gibberish and we won't get the key unless we have the password and fingerprint. Maybe my dad can help us figure this out in the morning." Claire turned in the chair. "We're both dead on our feet. Let's get some sleep."

Rafe didn't argue and he moved away from her quickly. *What's he thinking?*

"Lock the door once I leave," he instructed.

"I really think we're safe here."

"Humor me, okay?"

She nodded and stood so she could come around the desk and lock the door. When she was next to him, he took her hand. Claire smiled, glad he initiated the contact. "Night."

He stared down at her for a moment, but she couldn't hold his gaze. It was silly. She'd only known him for less than a day and she'd been reckless kissing him like that, but she still didn't regret it.

"'Night," was all he said as he squeezed her hand and left, softly shutting the door behind him.

Once he was gone, she locked herself in and walked to the cot. Kicking off her shoes she sat there silently for a moment, going over the events of the day. It had been one emotional extreme to the other and Claire was exhausted mentally and physically. She carefully laid down and curled her hands around the flat, little pillow. Her fingers stole to her lips.

What have I gotten myself into?

Chapter Eleven

Rafe slowly stretched out his uninjured shoulder, turning to look at the color patterns the stained glass windows left on the chapel floor. The higher the sun rose, the brighter the colors became. And was it his imagination or were all the blues and greens converging on the spot where he'd kissed Claire last night?

Even though he raised himself up as carefully as possible, his back scraped the wooden bench. The pain jolted him out of his thoughts. He had to get out of here. Vince's time was running out and he needed to make a plan, not lay here thinking about how Claire Michaels felt in his arms last night.

With a grimace he took the plastic bag the medic had given him out of the deep pocket of the sweatpants. His back probably needed some of that ointment and a bandage change. Then he'd wake Claire and tell her goodbye. It would be better that way.

Heading to the bathroom, he passed the closed office door, hesitating a bit. Part of him wanted to wake her up so they could spend a little more time together before he left. Resigned to the circumstances, he willed his feet to keep going. *Vince needs me.* He pushed into the little bathroom, opened the baggie, and began to set out the supplies on the edge of the sink. Gingerly pulling off his t-shirt, he looked in the mirror to take stock of his injuries. New cut on his forehead. Stitches on left side under his arm. Burns on his back. And his ever-aching knee. *Nothing that will kill me.*

Hearing a door close, he poked his head out. Claire was going down the hallway toward the chapel, carrying her gun belt in her hand. "Claire, I'm in here."

She turned immediately and came toward him. "I'm not interrupting a private moment, am I?"

He smiled. "No. Good morning." Her hair was tousled, as if she'd just rolled out of bed and finger-combed through it. The feel of it in his own fingers last night rose in his mind. *Like silk.* "Did you sleep well?" He clenched his hands so he wouldn't be tempted to reach out and touch it again.

"Let's just say morning came a little too quickly. How about you? Did you sleep at all?"

"Some." He motioned toward his back. "I'm trying to rebandage my back and get some ointment on it, but I'm having a tough time doing it myself. Feel like helping me?"

"Sure." She squeezed around him into the bathroom.

He turned to watch her, not realizing how much smaller the bathroom was with both of them in it. Should he stay where he was? Go back to the sink? She looked at him in the mirror as if trying to figure out what he was doing. His gaze fell on her bandage curling at the edges, giving him something to say that wouldn't make her feel awkward that he'd been staring at her. "I should probably take a look at your neck, too."

She didn't argue with him, just started getting a bit of gauze wet. "I think we should clean your burn up a bit before we put the ointment on."

Taking a step toward her, he looked down into her face, wishing he knew what she was thinking. "Good idea," he said softly.

Claire didn't meet his eyes, instead she busied herself by taking the antibiotic cream from him to set on the sink. She deftly turned him around so she could reach his back and began to remove the bandage the EMT had applied. Once it was off, she started to clean the area with the gauze. He watched her work in the mirror. "I think you missed your calling. You should have been a nurse or something."

"I thought about it when I was a kid. I was constantly bandaging up my brother's scrapes. He was the daredevil of the family, always jumping off fences and out of trees." She smiled as she concentrated on his wound. "Luke was going to save the world and I wanted to be right there with him."

He was quiet, the love for her brother so evident in her warm tone of voice. What could he say? "Luke was a hero, Claire. And you've obviously helped a lot of people in your profession," he said finally. "I know you've helped me."

She stopped her ministrations to meet his gaze in the mirror. Her eyes were searching, but for what, Rafe couldn't decide. "You know, I've never told anyone half the stuff I've told you. It's like you have this ability to get me to talk, when it's usually the other way around—*I* get people to talk." Her voice was light, but her eyes were serious.

"Your secrets are safe with me, Claire. Promise."

She reached over and grabbed the cream from the sink. He watched her in the mirror as she squeezed a bit out to make a design of little dots on his back, her touch so feather-light it made him want to tilt his head back and sigh. The cream was like little drops of water on the fire that was consuming part of his back.

"I think we're going to need to put it all over the burn, no matter how much it hurts," he said trying to stay still so she could finish.

"I know, but this is going to make it a little easier." Once she had dotted the entire area, she gently started to join the dots together, and before he knew it, the wound was covered. "How did you get all these other scars?"

"Motorcycle crash, parachute landing gone wrong, and falling down a mountainside."

"Adrenaline junkie or just clumsy?"

Rafe gave her his best are-you-kidding-me look in the mirror. "Neither."

She laughed, an infectious sound that made him want to join in.

He craned his neck to look at his now antibiotic-covered back. "That was really clever what you did with the cream."

"Thanks," she said with a smile as she started to re-bandage his back. "It was a trick my brother taught me to make it hurt less."

Rafe turned around, the small space bringing him within millimeters of Claire. He couldn't resist any longer and reached out to touch her hair. Her brown eyes flew to his. Suddenly, the bathroom seemed to close in around them and all he could see was her. "Claire."

She put her hand on his chest, but drew back when she touched his bare skin. "Rafe, I need to talk to you." She took a deep breath. "About last night."

Rafe leaned forward, his body brushing against Claire's as he grabbed his shirt off the back of the sink.

"Let me help you put that on," she said, as if relieved he was getting dressed. He pushed his head through and she helped him get his arms in without too much pull on his bandages. When he had his shirt on, she continued. "I want you to know I don't usually go around kissing people I've just met." To his surprise, he saw a blush rising in her cheeks. "It was just the events of the day, and the memories of Luke all rolling up into one moment." She looked up at him, her brown eyes troubled. "I felt like you understood me and I haven't had that in a really long time."

112

He brought his hands to her shoulders, letting his thumbs make lazy circles on her collarbone. "Claire, I've never met a woman like you before. You're fearless and you put yourself in harm's way to try to save others. You could have died yesterday and yet here you are trying to help me." His thumb lightly touched the bandage on her neck. "No matter what happens, I won't ever forget yesterday. Or you." He let his hands slide down her arms as she looked at the floor. "And for the record, I don't usually kiss people I've just met either."

She tilted her head to look up at him. She smiled. "Maybe it's because you're a SEAL after all. That would explain it."

He groaned. "Please forget I ever said that, okay?" He bent his head, his eyes never leaving hers. She licked her lips, and watched him, her eyes half-closing as he moved closer. Mustering all the self-control he had, he resisted the temptation to repeat last night and instead kissed her lightly on the forehead.

Rafe heard a little exhale as he pulled away. Was that from disappointment? Or relief?

"It's forgotten." She moved her hair over one shoulder. "Now it's your turn. While we've got all the bandages out and everything."

Rafe nodded. *Back to business.* He started to remove the soiled bandage, only stopping when she winced. Working quickly after that, he got the old bandage off and took a deep breath at the sight of the wound. He wasn't squeamish, but felt a little responsible that it had happened to her at all. "Does it hurt?"

"No." She closed her eyes.

"Liar." He chuckled. After putting on the fresh bandage, he leaned back to survey his work. "Much better. For two amateurs, I think we did a great job."

"Amateurs? Speak for yourself." A corner of her mouth turned up as if she were trying not to smile. "I'm sure I took a few classes in first aid, now that I think about it."

"Another seminar?" He smiled.

"Yeah, something like that."

She was about to say more, but Rafe heard an odd scraping sound coming from the back door area. "Do you hear that?" She nodded, tensing. "Stay here," he told her.

In a flash he was down the hall, but Claire ran past him, her gun at the ready. *What does she think she's doing?* He caught up, putting himself between her and the door. "I'll take point. Cover me."

"Stay out of the way, Rafe," she hissed, trying to move around him. "You'll only get yourself hurt and I'm the one with the gun."

The arguing stopped when they both saw the deadbolt turn. Rafe tensed. As the door slowly opened, a man's head appeared and Rafe pulled him through, slamming the door in case he wasn't alone. He made sure Claire was still behind him, gun in position, as he smashed the intruder against the wall face first, his forearm choking off any sound the man might make. He ground the man's cheek into the wall, glancing away for a moment. "Hand me your gun, Claire."

With the distraction, the man reared back, his skull connecting with Rafe's forehead, catching Rafe off-guard. He hunched over as the room spun for a moment, but quickly recovered, lunging for the man who was now scrambling toward the office.

"Stop," Claire shouted as she ran toward them. "Rafe, stop!"

Rafe caught the guy just as he put his hand on the office door. They grappled. Trying to get him pinned down again was proving difficult. He'd obviously been trained in hand-to-hand.

"Give me the gun, now!" Rafe shouted as he grabbed for the intruder one more time. *If she's not going to use it, I will.*

"Claire, it's me," the man said as Rafe landed a punch to the gut. The breath whooshed out of the guy and he dropped to the floor.

"Rafe stop!" Claire yelled again, moving forward. She knelt over the now prone man. "Dad? Are you okay?"

Dad. The word reverberated through Rafe's mind. Claire's dad? Had he just attacked the Chief of the National Clandestine Service? *Uh oh.*

Claire helped her dad into the office and Rafe followed. Once the door was shut, she turned on the light, shouldering her father's weight. He collapsed on the chair near the desk. "What's going on here?" he wheezed.

"I'm sorry, sir. After the last twenty-four hours I thought you might be an enemy. I guess it wasn't clear . . . " Rafe wasn't sure how to explain.

"I wasn't expecting you to come in person." Claire knelt in front of her father. "You were supposed to call."

Rafe felt a little better that she didn't seem angry at him. He touched his forehead, glad his earlier cut hadn't re-opened considering the force of the hit he'd taken.

"I needed to get to you. You don't realize the full scope of the situation." Claire's father held out his hand. "You must be Rafe Kelly. I'm Skip Michaels. You pack quite a punch." There was a grudging admiration in his tone.

Rafe shook his hand and pointed to his head. "Thank you, sir. I was just thinking you have quite a hard head."

Skip laughed and leaned forward, one hand still on his abdomen. "You're probably wondering what I'm doing here."

"Sir?"

"I listened to the tapes of the negotiation on the roof yesterday and spent most of the night trying to figure out what's really going on. This is definitely tied to al-Qaeda, but I think you know that." Skip faced Rafe head on. "Am I right?"

Rafe glanced at Claire. "Bez Ruhallah got hold of a Black Widow and used it to try to get Gary's encryption key of the last bin

Laden. When Bez couldn't get his hands on it himself, he took my brother and is offering an exchange at the Intercontinental Hotel in Kabul. I'm supposed to meet him there the day after tomorrow."

"Did Bez say anything else to you?"

"Not really. Well, he did say that if he can't have the file, he doesn't want the Americans to have it. And that the file will help him rebuild bin Laden's empire." Rafe leaned forward, rubbing his chin. "I have to admit I was pretty surprised to see him. With the information he was privy to in the al-Qaeda organization, I would think you guys would have had him under lock and key for a long time."

"To make the story short, no one knows for sure what happened. There's a lot of finger-pointing going on right now. As for getting back into the country undetected, we think he had some help. There's no other explanation for how he got in with that sort of weaponry."

"Do you know who would help him?" Claire sat on the edge of the desk.

"We're working some angles and I spent most of the night speccing out an op so we can smoke him out. And get your brother back." Skip stood. "I have a presidential order to keep it with my team for now. And believe me, that wasn't easy." He walked to the door. "Do you have the encryption key?"

Rafe nodded. "Do you have any idea what's on it? Claire and I tried to take a look last night, but it needs a password and Gary's fingerprint."

Skip turned and started to pace in front of the desk. "When SEAL Team Six found the compound where bin Laden was, they confiscated several computers. The DoD has been working on them ever since, but there was one file they couldn't crack. We knew Axis had been working on a data recovery program that was advanced enough we thought it could do what DoD couldn't. Looks like we were right."

"But why is this particular file so important?" Claire put her hand on her father's arm, stopping his pacing with her question.

"From some of the other files we saw, we think this is the Holy Grail of the al-Qaeda network—that the file details every sleeper cell and sleeper agent that is in America. If we could decrypt it, we could round them up and possibly cut off the head of the beast. That's why Bez doesn't want America to have it, but if he could get it, well, it would *definitely* help him rebuild what bin Laden was working for."

The flash drives in Rafe's pocket were starting to take on a whole different meaning. "If Axis was given something so important to national security, why weren't they being protected?"

Skip started pacing again. "We had light surveillance going on and one man posted on the inside so as to not give ourselves away by making a big deal of it. But Bez came at us with no warning at all, no chatter, no nothing. Using the bomb was ingenious because there wasn't anything we could do. It was over before it started. Not to mention investigating the hostage situation was a great distraction while your brother was being kidnapped."

"Why wouldn't Gary tell someone what was on that file if he saw it?"

"It was probably pretty detailed. He went to your brother for protection the morning he was killed. Vince had put in a call to his DoD contact, but before they could get anything in place, it was over."

"If we can't crack the file without Gary, then Bez won't be able to, either, right?" Claire asked, rubbing her temples, obviously trying to process the information.

Skip glanced at Rafe. "If only it were that simple. I think it's only a matter of time, but that's something Vince doesn't have. And we can't afford to have that file exposed under any circumstances."

Rafe understood that look. "They're going to kill Vince unless I give them the file. I'm not just going to let him die."

"I want to do everything I can to make sure that doesn't happen, but you can understand how reluctant we are to hand the file over to Bez." Skip didn't mince words. "Every government agency in the U.S. is in an uproar over this. It's the opportunity of a lifetime to stick a stake in al-Qaeda's heart and possibly save American lives."

"But they think sacrificing Vince's life is an acceptable option." Rafe's voice sounded bitter to his ears, but he knew how these things worked. "There's got to be a better way."

"Not one that benefits Vince."

Rafe's stomach sank. "I'll go after him myself then. I know where Bez hides."

Skip put his hand on Rafe's arm. "That's why I'm here. I want to help you." He turned to Claire, put his arm around her, and squeezed. "I know what it's like to feel helpless when someone you love is in danger half a world away."

Rafe let out a breath of relief. "What do you have planned?"

"You're going to have to trust me, son. Completely. Right now." He walked to the door and opened it. "Are you in?"

Chapter Twelve

Claire was tired. More tired than she could ever remember being. Her father had immediately taken them to the airport and they had gotten on a private plane to New York where they'd picked up Sam Shelton, a computer expert. All of them had to run for the connecting flight to Dubai where they'd caught one more flight to Kabul. So within just a few hours of waking up that morning, they were crossing the ocean to Afghanistan. Sometimes it did pay to have a dad with connections.

So far things had been all business between Claire and her father. She'd sort of expected it, but a small part of her always hoped it would be different. Her father wasn't a touchy feely sort of guy no matter how hard Claire wished for it. He was a definitely a bottom-line type. Always had been, probably always would be. It was just hard to accept sometimes.

Claire looked over at Rafe. He was sitting with Sam poring over the flash drives almost in the same position he had been since the plane took off. He hadn't shown any signs of slowing down and only occasionally stopped to stretch his back. *I wonder how his back is really feeling.*

They hadn't had any time alone together since her father showed up and Claire was anxious to ask him how he was doing with all this. Having a brother in captivity was a kind of anguish no one could imagine who hadn't been there themselves. But, from the look of things, Rafe dealt with high stress like she usually did—he wanted to work through it or keep himself so busy he didn't have time to think about it. Claire knew how valuable it was to have someone to talk to and she wanted to be there for Rafe.

"Can't you sleep?" her father asked from the seat next to her.

"No." She shifted to the side deciding to just dive into what she needed to say about their family. "Have you called Will recently? He's having problems at school, you know."

Her father rubbed his neck. "I've called, but he won't talk to me. I know he's upset about me moving back to Washington without them, but I didn't have a choice."

"I'm not accusing, Dad, just telling you what I know. He's cutting class to play a video game with his friend. He thinks you don't love him because he's not Luke."

"He told you that?" Her dad's eyes looked pained. "I've never said anything like that."

"I think he's just trying to figure out where he fits into your life, that's all." Claire bit her lip. "Do you think you can convince Marlene to move to Washington?"

"I don't know. Everything is a mess right now. She wants to be close to her mother and for Will to be able to finish school. He's transferred so many times, she wants some stability for him, which I totally understand. But she wants to stay in Hartford for another year at least and I can't really take a hiatus from my job. She's making this an all or nothing ultimatum."

"Have you ever thought of retiring?"

"A lot more lately." He tilted his head to look out the window. "But I still feel like I have something to offer my country. Especially at times like this."

"Do you mean with someone being kidnapped by al-Qaeda? Like Luke?" Her voice was soft. "How have you been coping? Did you ever see a grief counselor?"

His posture was upright, aloof, just like him. After she spoke, the space between them seemed magnified somehow and she didn't know how to breach it. Luke's death should have drawn them closer, not put a wedge between them. She couldn't let it go so easily. "Dad?"

"It's been three years, Claire. I'm fine." He looked up as Rafe approached. "Get anything?"

"Yeah, we found Gary's back door. I knew he would have one."

"What do you mean?" Claire asked, sitting up straighter. It would change the game if they knew exactly what was on the file.

"We can bypass the password, but it needs another fingerprint."

Claire raised her eyebrows. "Whose?"

"Vince's. So if we can find Vince, we can get his fingerprint on there and decrypt the file."

"You make it sound so easy." Skip ran a hand over his barely visible hairline. "Does Bez know this? Is that why he has Vince?"

"I don't think so. It sounded like he wanted to make an exchange." Rafe sat down across the aisle from them. "Are you ready to fill me in on your plan?"

"I will as soon as the team is assembled. They're meeting us at Camp Eggers."

"Who's on the team?" Rafe asked.

"I've got at least one from your SEAL team," Skip said. "And a few added members."

Rafe smiled. "If you've got any people from my team, sir, then we're in good hands."

Skip motioned to the shirt Rafe was wearing. "Did you go to the Naval Academy?"

Claire chewed on her lip. She didn't know how her dad would react since she thought he'd be further along in the grief process by now, but she knew she had to tell him. Worried, she looked from her dad to Rafe and back. "He was in an explosion and his clothes were shredded. I offered him something of Luke's."

Her dad looked at the t-shirt for a long moment, then slowly turned his gaze to her and waited until she met it. "You gave him Luke's Naval Academy t-shirt? His favorite?"

"I'm sorry if that hurt you, but you know Luke would have been the first to offer it if he were here."

"But he isn't here, is he?"

"We can't hold onto his things forever, Dad. He's not coming home. He doesn't need it."

Their gazes locked once more, the tension palpable until he stood and walked toward the back of the plane. Claire watched him go. She hadn't realized how much he was still struggling with her brother's loss. She'd thought, or at least hoped, that time would heal it or he would reach out for help. Apparently, he hadn't.

She rolled her neck and saw how uncomfortable Rafe looked. "I'm sorry, Rafe. I didn't even think my father would mind. He's still having a hard time with losing Luke."

"Some losses are impossible to get over. I'm sure seeing Luke's shirt brought back memories for him." He looked down at his chest. "Maybe I should find something else to wear."

"Really, it's fine. Luke would have given anyone in need the shirt off his back and you were definitely in need." She gave a small wave in Sam's direction. "Besides, where else would you get something to wear? Are you going to trade shirts with Sam? He's probably about half your size. I don't think his t-shirt would fit you and yours would look like a dress on him."

Rafe smiled. "Well, when you put it that way." He moved into the seat next to hers and sat down carefully, mindful of his back. "Is everything okay? Things seem tense with you and your dad."

"No, it's not that. He was gone a lot when I was a kid so I don't really know him that well. We're just . . . well, we're working on things."

Rafe took that into consideration. "So he probably has regrets about not being there for Luke and then having him die like that."

His insight surprised her. "I hadn't thought of it like that before."

Rafe intertwined his fingers with hers. "Regrets are a hard thing to live with." He ran his thumb over the back of her hand so softly, it was almost a caress.

Is he talking about my dad or us? "Do you have any regrets?"

"Too many." He turned in his seat, but didn't let go of her hand. "You know, you look exhausted. You should try and get some sleep."

"Thanks," she said wryly. "For some reason I have a lot on my mind."

"There's nothing you can do until we land. Why don't you take advantage of the downtime?"

"I could ask you the same thing. Have you slept more than an hour or two since we left New York?"

"I can't sleep or eat when I'm worried," he confided. "And Bez isn't exactly known for his humanity. Vince isn't used to this kind of thing. I have too many scenarios going through my head about what might be happening to him." He took a deep breath and let it out slowly.

Claire nodded. "I do that, too—think of every scenario that can happen when I'm called on a case, and then I try to predict reactions and outcomes. It can drain you."

"How do you get through it?"

123

She looked over at his worried face, wishing she could fix it for him, or that her words could comfort him somehow. "I think of the happiest outcome. Let that be my guide."

He leaned his head against the backrest, his face inches from hers. The pull she felt toward him was more powerful the more time she spent with him. She squeezed his fingers and he brought her hand to his lips. "Maybe I'll try that."

Warmth spread through her, starting at her hand where he'd kissed her. Wishing they had more time alone, she almost frowned when she heard her father coming up the aisle. Claire gave Rafe a half-smile instead. "Thanks for listening. Again. I swear I need to figure out your technique for getting so much information out of me. Maybe you should consider hostage negotiations when your military career is over." Too late she remembered his knee injury and the fact that his military career *could* very well be over. She inwardly cringed at her careless words. "I'm sorry, Rafe, I didn't meant it like that."

As her father took the last steps to their seats, Rafe nodded and let go of her fingers. "I think I'm going to go try to sleep. You should try, too. Seriously."

"I will." Claire mentally kicked herself as he stood and left. *What's wrong with me?*

She watched him go back to Sam, reaching into the overhead bin on his way to grab a blanket and pillow. *I'm tired, that's all.* Sleep would help her get back to her normal clear-headed self and provide the oblivion she wanted right now. Curling up toward the window, she leaned against the cool glass, hoping she would fall asleep quickly. *Think of the best scenario. Good thoughts.*

Her dad sat down next to her again, taking the seat Rafe had vacated. "Claire, this could get dangerous. Maybe I made a mistake letting you come along."

The warmth she felt a moment ago disappeared as Claire turned to him, incredulous. "*Letting* me come along? You make me sound like I'm a child."

"You're *my* child." He frowned at her, obviously annoyed she didn't go along with his assessment.

"Dad, I deal with dangerous situations every day. You know that. It's what I'm trained for. You brought me along for my skills in hostage negotiations and for the fact that you can trust me. Isn't that what you said?"

"Maybe your safety is more important."

She sighed.

"That reminds me, Captain Reed approved your leave of absence, but he said he wants it short and he wants you home safe and sound so be careful." He shook his head. "Maybe he has the right idea."

"Dad, are you sure you wanting me to go home all of the sudden doesn't have something to do with me giving Luke's clothes to Rafe and asking you about how you've dealt with your grief?"

He stared at the back of the seat in front of him. "I know he's not coming back, Claire. But I would give anything if I could see him one more time. Anything. And I don't want to lose you, too." He took a deep breath as if saying those words had cost him something.

Claire held in her surprise. "You're not going to lose me, Dad." She patted his arm. "Everything will be fine. We've got it taken care of. You'll see."

With a glance over at Rafe who now had his back to her, she stared for a moment then closed her eyes. "I'm going to try to get some sleep. I think we all need some rest."

Her dad didn't say anything for several seconds and she was tempted to open one eye to see what he was doing, but she resisted. Finally, he leaned over and kissed the top of her head, waited half a heartbeat, then stood and left.

Claire felt her eyes fill with tears and opened them. Discreetly wiping her cheeks, she looked over to see Rafe watching her. Giving him a smile, she curled her body back toward the small window again. When had everything gotten so complicated?

Chapter Thirteen

Rafe knew he'd be coming back to Afghanistan eventually, but he certainly hadn't thought it would be under these circumstances. He looked out the window. He'd never seen anything like it. The view from that altitude made the mountains and valleys surrounding Kabul look like an old man's wrinkly hand, with the city at center.

They circled like a bird eyeing prey, the airport growing larger as they approached. After a bumpy landing they coasted to a stop. As soon as the door opened, Rafe moved toward it, anxious to get going. He needed to do something for his brother. He'd tried to stay calm on the outside, but the waiting was driving him crazy.

He stepped off the plane and walked down the steps to the tarmac. From the looks of it, Afghanistan was the same way he'd left it—dusty and brown. Glancing up to see where Claire was, he saw that her father was right at her side as they descended the steps. It was evident Claire loved her dad from the way she looked at him. The issues between them were obviously deep, but Claire sounded hopeful they could be worked out. He liked that about her—she was optimistic about everything. *That probably helps her a lot in her job*, he thought.

As he looked out over the dingy airfield, he was grateful to be doing something instead of sitting. All his muscles were ready to get this mission going. Get Vince. Get home.

He moved away from the bottom of the stairs and waited for Skip and Claire. They stood together in a half-circle. Skip shaded his eyes, looking off into the distance, as if expecting someone. They didn't have to wait long for a car to appear as a black Toyota Land Cruiser headed down the airfield toward them. "Looks like our ride made it," Skip commented.

Rafe squinted, trying to get a look at the driver, but couldn't with the tinted windows. Whomever was driving was flooring it. He was in front of them in less than three minutes. When he opened the door, he came around to greet them. "Rafe Kelly. Bet you didn't think you'd see me again."

The shock of red hair and quiet demeanor gave him away in an instant. Rafe had never met anyone else with hair as red as Patrick's or with a less friendly demeanor. "Patrick, what are you doing here? I thought you'd still be stuck out in Paktika province."

Patrick shook his head, clasping his hands behind his back. "Thankfully I was sent to Kabul. It's nice to have some semblance of civilization." He looked around. "You got any luggage?"

"No, it was sort of a last minute thing."

Patrick's eyes drifted behind Rafe and from the wolfish smile on his face, Rafe knew he'd spotted Claire. "And you are?"

Rafe turned. "Claire Michaels, this is Patrick Daynes."

"Nice to meet you." Claire held out her hand and Patrick shook it.

"Gentleman, I hate to break up this little reunion, but we've got work to do." Skip didn't wait for any reply after he spoke, he merely climbed in back of the SUV. "Sam, get that equipment loaded in the back."

Patrick gave Rafe a look. "The Chief's right. I heard this is about your brother. I'm sorry, Rafe."

"We're going to get him back," Rafe opened the car door, surprised to see another man in the back. "Oh, sorry, I didn't realize you were there." He was wearing an Afghan army uniform with a lot of medals on it.

Skip made the introduction from the front passenger seat. "This is Deputy Commander Ludin from the Afghan Special Forces. He's got all our clearances so we're free to go to Camp Eggers."

"Nice to meet you," Rafe replied. The man looked angry, staring straight ahead, barely acknowledging Rafe. With a raise of his eyebrows, Rafe gave Claire a look of surprise before he got in. *Well, this is awkward.*

It was a silent ride to the city, although Patrick maneuvered the streets of Kabul like a pro. There weren't traffic rules like the States and the streets were almost always congested. There were a lot of people everywhere, but it just felt muted—sort of like New York, but without any of its color or energy. A brown Big Apple. The crowds would make it easy for someone to disappear in, which was probably why Bez had chosen it. Rafe turned away from the window, but the view wasn't much better inside the car. He could just barely see the top of Claire's head where she was crammed in between her father and Patrick. *I wonder what she thinks of Afghanistan so far.*

After hitting every muddy pothole on the road, Patrick finally made it to the front gate of Camp Eggers. Within a few moments, they were ushered inside. Rafe looked around at the courtyard area, complete with tables and chairs and a coffee shop. It looked more like Shangri-la compared to the more primitive outpost he'd left in Paktika on the Pakistan border. But he didn't have much time to compare as Skip kept up a steady pace and headed immediately to a far office.

Skip took command as soon as they entered and crowded around a small table. "I'm happy to meet all of you face-to-face finally." He pointed to the man next to him who had met them at the gate. "This is Commander Tom Cooper. He's helping me coordinate this op." He shifted around to the head of the table as Tom greeted everyone.

When it quieted down, Tom assumed an at-ease stance, legs apart, his hands behind his back. "If it's okay with you, Chief, I'd like to start our status report with Deputy Commander Ludin."

Ludin gave a nod of acknowledgment before he started speaking. "We've swept the Intercontinental hotel and there's been no sign of Bez Ruhallah. It doesn't seem credible to me that he would tell you to meet him at the Intercontinental. It is one of the best guarded hotels in the city."

"Maybe he's got inside help." Rafe rubbed his brow, feeling annoyed at Ludin's implication that he wasn't credible. "Did any U.S. personnel accompany you on your sweep?"

"I don't need any U.S. personnel to help me sweep a hotel in my own country." Ludin barely controlled the anger in his voice.

"Would your men really tell us if Bez had been spotted?" Rafe felt just as angry. Maybe the inside help was from right here inside the team. Gary had said not to trust anyone before he died.

Ludin stood straight, turning to face Rafe head on. "I don't like what you're implying. Do you think we want al-Qaeda or any foreign entities in our country?"

Rafe raised himself to his full height and stared Ludin down. "Just so we're clear, the U.S. is doing its best to help your country. And I'm sure we'll be leaving just as soon as we possibly can."

Claire had been standing by the door and Rafe saw her move toward him out of the corner of his eye. "It won't do any good to fight amongst ourselves." She joined him, facing Ludin. "We just want to make sure Rafe's brother gets home safely, that's all."

Ludin twisted his head toward Skip. "Should he really be involved in this if he is so emotional?"

Rafe took a step forward, his hands clenched into fists. "Don't even try that with me. That's my brother out there."

Claire moved just an inch closer so that their shoulders were touching, giving him silent support. "Bez specifically asked for Rafe so if he doesn't show, Bez will know something's wrong. We can't afford to spook him."

Skip put up his hand. "Rafe is going and we'll be covering him." He tilted his head toward Rafe. "And we all have to trust each other here."

Rafe folded his arms and leaned back against the wall, embracing his shoulder pain to release some of the anger. Claire adjusted to his new position so she was still right next to him. It was comforting to have her there. She seemed to be the only one on his side.

Tom continued. "From our end we were able to track the plane Bez used to get in and out of the States. It's exactly what you thought, Chief," he said. "Bez has teamed up with the Gulf drug cartel. According to our sources, there's a deal being made to amp up Bez's old Afghan heroin ring, ship the product to Mexico and funnel it to the cartel's distribution lanes inside the U.S. It has the potential to be a multi-billion dollar deal if Bez can really get product to them."

"Who's leading the cartel these days?" Skip asked, putting a hand on his temple as if he were feeling the beginning of a headache.

"Luis Chapa."

Rafe's head was spinning with the information he'd just heard. "So al-Qaeda and a Mexican cartel teamed up against the U.S.? Is that what you're saying?"

"That's exactly what I'm saying. We've suspected that al-Qaeda was making an alliance with them, but this is our first real evidence." Skip pivoted in his seat and crossed one leg over the other.

The little wooden chair obviously wasn't that comfortable. "The Gulf cartel is known for their violence and that would appeal to Bez. I'm guessing that's how they smuggled your brother out of the country as well without any flags coming up. Their Texas shipping lanes especially are ever-changing and tough to find."

Rafe ran a hand through his hair. This was worse than he'd thought. *An al-Qaeda alliance with a cartel?* It was a logical way to infiltrate the U.S., but it made Rafe's blood run cold at the thought of trying to fight it. "What's in this for Bez besides a lot of money?"

"We think he's looking to take bin Laden's place in al-Qaeda and he would need funding and a show of strength. The drug money would provide the funding and if he carries out the attack on that file, he's got a position of strength. It would probably clinch his leadership spot." Tom's words were matter-of-fact, just like his demeanor.

"Which is why we can't give him the chance to carry out any attack," Ludin put in. "Destroy the encryption key. Let whatever is on it die with bin Laden and say good riddance. It will keep my nation safe for the price of one American life."

Skip stood at Ludin's words. "Commander Ludin, you are here to provide us with tactical support. If you don't feel that you can set aside your personal feelings about foreign entities in your country, I will understand and you can step aside. We can have our own personnel take up the slack."

"Best idea I've heard all day," Rafe said under his breath. He felt Claire's elbow in his side. "Well, it's true," he whispered.

"I will try to be more circumspect with my personal opinions," Ludin said, with a slight bow.

"Can't we just figure out the encryption ourselves so we can prevent the attack and give Bez a fake one?" Patrick spoke up, his voice hopeful.

"Bez told me he had an idea of what was on the plans and he would know a fake. Besides, Gary put several security measures in place, including fingerprints and we don't have the time to crack it before we meet with Bez." Rafe ran his hand over his head. "What's the plan here, Chief?"

Skip looked around the circle of men at the table. "We're going to go up to the hotel, just like was agreed. We'll have a team covering you, Rafe, and when we have your brother in the clear, we'll grab Bez."

Rafe shook his head immediately. "That will put my brother at risk. I don't want him in the middle."

"We're a highly trained unit. There won't be a middle."

Ludin turned to Rafe. "Do you have the encryption key?"

Rafe warily nodded.

"I'd like to see what's on it, these security protocols you mentioned. Perhaps our men can help with it." His tone was even and his eyes stared straight into Rafe's.

"I think we've got that covered, but thanks," Rafe said. There was no way he was giving that key up to anyone. It meant the difference between his brother's life and his death.

"We can't just hand over that key to Bez. It's taking a mighty big chance with our national security if we do." Patrick's face was tense, his lips pressed together.

"We're well aware of the risks," Skip said. "If everything goes according to plan, there won't be any national security issues."

"We can't even secure Camp Eggers," Patrick continued as if Skip hadn't spoken. "Just last month one of our SUVs was stolen with a laptop inside that had classified information on it. How do you think they got the specs for that rooftop bomb Bez set off?"

"Quiet, Daynes," Skip ordered.

Rafe turned to his friend, then whirled back around to confront Skip. "Is that how they got the specs for that bomb?" Rafe asked. "Did you know about this? If it was stolen a month ago, why didn't we do something? Warn someone? Gary could still be alive!"

"We're investigating what happened," Skip told him. "Your concern is your brother. Stick to that."

Rafe felt like the walls were closing in on him. He had to get out of there. "Excuse me." He moved toward the door, suppressing the urge to push everyone out of the way.

"Where do you think you're going, Lieutenant?" Skip called.

"I need some air." He pulled open the door. "I'm not going to miss my deadline with Bez. With or without you, I'm going to that hotel."

Breathing deeply once he was outside, he stalked over to a corner table in the courtyard and sat down. Everything about the military was ordered, right down to how they served meals. Yet everything that had happened in the last three days was anything but ordered. Rafe needed to get a handle on it, fast. It felt like he was losing his mind, all his senses on overload.

He took another deep breath. A shadow fell across his table and he looked up to find Claire standing over him. "Come on," she invited. "I want to show you something."

He took her hand, the warmth of it in his own the best thing that had happened to him all day.

"Where are we going?"

"Right here." She pulled him into a little alley between two buildings and wrapped her arms around his waist, being careful of his injuries. "You looked like you could use a friend."

He didn't say anything, just held her close to him. Dropping his head to her shoulder, he turned his face into her neck and breathed in her scent. "Thank you."

After a few minutes she pulled back. "We'll go to the hotel and ask for proof of life. If we get it, then you can give them the encryption key. We'll get Vince out of there before Bez knows what's happened. Then the team will grab him and we'll all be home safe before you know it."

Rafe immediately shook his head, taking her by the shoulders, remembering how she strode across the roof, ready for anything. It seemed like a lifetime ago now. "I don't want you there, Claire. It's too dangerous. I can do this. I can wear a wire and you can talk me through it on an earpiece."

Claire stepped back with a frown. "I'm a cop, Rafe. A hostage negotiator. This is a hostage negotiation. *I'm* the one who should be there."

He rubbed a hand over his face, too tired to argue and too afraid to really delve into the myriad feelings he had toward this woman. "I don't want you hurt, Claire."

"I don't want *you* hurt. So we'll both stay safe." She took a step away and reached back for him, her hand outstretched. "We've got to get back. They want us both wired and ready."

Rafe took her hand and pulled her close again, not quite ready to go. She seemed to understand, and reached up on her tiptoes to lightly kiss him on the lips. Rafe closed his eyes for a split second as she pulled his head down to speak softly in his ear. "Trust me. We're going to get through this. Best case scenario, remember?"

He hugged her, hoping she was right. *I really need her to be right because if she isn't . . . If this ends like it did for Luke . . .* Rafe couldn't finish the thought. "Let's go."

Chapter Fourteen

Claire clutched the chadari covering her head as she read Bez's psych profile one more time. With the information they had, it indicated that Bez was self-centered, manipulative, and possibly a sociopath. He was recruited to bin Laden's cause as a teenager and had worked his way up the organization by doing anything that was asked of him, but when he was in U.S. custody the evidence against him had been ruled circumstantial and he'd been released. Claire made a noise of frustration. If only . . .

Fingering the mic underneath her shirt collar, she went over the plan in her head one more time. She would accompany Rafe to the hotel. When Bez appeared they would tell him no deal until they had proof of life. If he produced Vince then the exchange would take place and, if possible, Bez would be grabbed before he left the grounds. If not, they would have to postpone the exchange and leave, telling Bez to bring proof of life or no deal.

But there were so many things that could go wrong and she was having a hard time imagining the best-case scenario.

Smoothing down her clothing, she bent over to check her ankle holster. They'd decided to go in armed, but concealed. Hopefully they wouldn't need it, but it was best to be prepared. She'd also been given a belt with a tracker in it. Rafe had one in his boots. If anything went wrong, the backup team would know their location and could get to them quickly. In this volatile situation, that provided a lot of comfort for Claire. Bez was unpredictable.

Patrick opened the door to the office, his eyes widening in surprise. "Are you ready? We're loading up."

Claire stood, closing the file in front of her. "Just going over things one more time. Doing a final check." She put her earpiece in. Everyone would be connected on this op.

Patrick moved closer and reached out to pat her arm. "Don't worry. Rafe will be right next to you and if he's not then I will be. You'll be covered."

She took a step back to tuck her chair under the table. "I know, but there are a lot of variables in this scenario."

"Hey, don't get pessimistic on me." He scrunched down to meet her eyes, his hands in his pants pockets. "A beautiful mouth like that shouldn't have a frown on it." He leaned in, his face so close she could smell the mint on his breath. "You want to change your mind about going?"

"If you *have* changed your mind, I need to know right now." Rafe stood in the open doorway, filling the entire space with his hands on his hips. "Hope I'm not interrupting anything."

Claire clutched the back of her chair a second longer, her gaze turned to Rafe. He was dressed in desert cammies that showed off his physique far better than the t-shirt and sweats he'd had on previously. "No, Patrick and I were just going over the plan one more time." She took a step toward the door.

"I was just assuring Claire that if you aren't with her, I will be." Patrick smiled at Rafe and folded his arms. "Right?"

Rafe turned on his heel, his expression as stormy as the day Claire had met him on the roof. "We're ready to go," he said gruffly.

He reached his hand back for Claire. Puzzled, Claire took it and he guided her out of the office, picking up the pace significantly as they walked through the courtyard.

Claire hurried to keep up with his long strides. "What's wrong?"

He glanced down at her, then briefly twisted his head around to look behind them. "We're in Afghanistan, meeting a terrorist to bargain for my brother's life. Do you really have to ask?"

"You seem distracted." She pushed her head covering back so she could see him clearly. "I need to know you're focused."

"That's not fair," he practically growled as he dropped her hand and headed off toward the three waiting SUVs. "You should worry about your own focus. We leave in five minutes," he said over his shoulder.

Patrick came up behind her and Claire wondered how much of their conversation he'd overheard. "He always was the jealous type."

Claire turned, surprised. *What is he getting at?* "Jealous? What would Rafe have to be jealous of?"

He grinned at her. "I don't know. Just making an observation."

Claire faced front to watch Rafe's retreating back. "He's just worried about his brother, that's all."

"If you say so." Patrick walked her to the lead vehicle. When they got there, he reached out to give her arm a squeeze. "See you at the hotel."

Claire got in the back passenger door, surprised to see Rafe get in the back as well. Her dad rode up front with Patrick. Even though she was wearing the chadari as a courtesy, she was glad to have it now. She rearranged it, keeping her hands busy and her eyes forward. Maybe Rafe was the kind of guy who needed space before an op. When she was working she didn't like a lot of extra chatter. It was just a matter of learning everyone's idiosyncracies in the field.

They got caught in a traffic jam on the way up to the hotel and stopped at two checkpoints. Judging by Rafe's bouncing knee he was frustrated with the delay. She leaned over and was going to say something, but thought the better of it and straightened again.

"You okay?" he asked, finally acknowledging her presence.

"I was about to ask you the same thing," she confessed. "You seem nervous."

"What makes you think that?"

She pointed to his knee. "Always a telltale sign."

He stopped bouncing. "I'm worried about making Bez's deadline," he admitted.

"Bez wants the encryption key. He'll wait."

Rafe leaned closer, moving the chadari aside to whisper in her ear. "Claire, I have a bad feeling about this. I can't explain it, but I want you to keep the key. When I signal, you can give it to me and I'll make the exchange, but for now, I want someone I trust carrying this." He took her hand, surreptitiously handing her the small drive.

She took it and put it in her pants pocket. "Are you sure about this? If you feel like something's not right, maybe we should call if off and regroup."

"What could I say? I have a feeling?" He shook his head. "We've got to go forward, but I want to be prepared."

Claire's stomach twisted into knots. His words rattled her more than she cared to admit. Before she had time to question him further, they pulled up in front of the hotel. Her father nodded to her as she exited. Rafe came around the car and took her elbow. "This is it."

The car drove off and Claire walked into the hotel lobby past several armed guards. "At least they're on top of security."

Rafe grimaced. "Hopefully they're not on Bez's payroll."

The fading light cast shadows on the check-in desk, giving the thin red carpet underneath her feet a blood-red hue. *Maybe it's a sign.* But as soon as she thought it, she put it out of her mind. *Stop it*, she chided. *Get on your game.*

Rafe approached the desk and the man behind it. "Hello, I'm Rafe Kelly. Do you speak English?" The man nodded. "You have a message for me?"

They waited while the man checked. Rafe turned to nonchalantly make a sweep of the lobby and Claire's gaze followed his. The large open space looked like it had been redone since the attack on it a few years earlier. The only feature that really was the same as it had been since the hotel was built were the wide columns in the middle of the room. From the look of the security guards they'd passed, the hotel owners had also taken precautions against another attack. *Why would Bez pick to meet here?*

The desk clerk came back with a small white envelope. "Yes, you have a message, sir."

Claire inched closer to Rafe as he opened the envelope. "Go to Room 488." *This could be a trap*, Claire thought as he bent it toward her to make sure she read it.

Rafe didn't show any outward reaction of his thoughts. He leaned over to the desk clerk. "I'd like a room, please. Room 488 if it's available."

The man looked at his lists. "Yes, it has been paid for already in your name." He took a card key out of a drawer. "Here you are, sir. Do you have any luggage?"

"No," Rafe said, his voice curt. "Thank you."

They crossed back the way they'd come, quietly waiting for the elevator.

"Go to the room," Skip directed through their earpieces. "Patrick will stay on the main floor and monitor it for any sign of Bez. Ludin has the perimeter."

141

Rafe and Claire both checked the elevator before getting in. When the doors opened on the fourth floor, Rafe took a step out, but Claire put her hand on his chest so she could get by him and make sure the coast was clear. She held in a smile at his annoyed look when she motioned him forward. Rafe kept his eyes open, obviously ready for anything, just like she was. When they came to 488, they stopped on either side of the door.

"Ready?" Rafe asked.

She nodded. He put in the key, slowly opening it. He kept his body to the side, his hand over his holster, ready to draw if necessary. Claire was right behind him as they went in. She checked the small bathroom and met Rafe in the middle of the suite. "All clear," he reported.

"Yeah." Claire looked around. "Now what?"

Rafe started looking under the bed and couch, pulling the drawer out of the tiny table. "There's got to be something more here. This is like a game to Bez. He's not going to leave us hanging for long." As soon as he finished speaking he held up a flat white box from the drawer. "I knew it." His hand trembled slightly as if he'd imagined some worst-case scenario of what could be in that box.

"Let me," she said, taking the box from him. Hoping to spare him pain, she opened it, determined to keep her reaction neutral. It was a note with a picture inside. Unfolding the note, she smoothed it out, then began to read. "Here's proof your brother is still alive. Put the encryption key in this box and bring it to the ballroom. You have ten minutes. Once the information is verified, you will be given directions to your brother's location." Claire held up the picture. It was of a disheveled Vince, his clothes torn, his cheek obviously bruised, holding a newspaper with yesterday's date plainly visible.

Rafe took the paper and picture from her hand. He stared for a long moment. "He looks okay overall, doesn't he? Or at least he was yesterday."

"Yes, he looks like he's holding up." She went to the window and looked out. Was Bez watching them? Was he even here? "What are you going to do?"

"All I know is I'm not leaving here without my brother." He paced to the window and back.

"Go to the ballroom. Patrick hasn't seen Bez, but we'll keep looking." Skip's voice was loud and clear in the earpiece.

"Do you really think he's nearby? Would he risk that?"

"He would want to be here. He craves attention." Rafe's voice was sarcastic as he holstered his gun once again. He moved next to her in the window, looking down at the view. "Are you sure you're okay?"

Claire was glad he hadn't mentioned Luke's name. Not with the entire team listening. "It feels good to be doing something this time instead of just waiting around, you know what I mean?"

He nodded. Pushing her chadari back onto her shoulders, he gave her a silent kiss on her forehead. "We should go."

They walked down the hall and took the elevator back to the lobby. With a few more turns, they made it to the ballroom where there was a small sign announcing some sort of meeting going on. *International Journalists Association.*

Claire bit her cheek. "Dad, any sign of Bez? There's a journalist event going on in the ballroom. If he's here, it could get ugly. Can we clear the room somehow?"

"Patrick, why didn't you tell us there was something going on in the ballroom?"

Silence greeted them. "Patrick?"

Claire put a hand to her earpiece, straining to hear Patrick's voice. Had Bez gotten hold of him? She walked through the ballroom door with Rafe at her side. When it was slammed shut behind her, she jumped. One of the security guards they'd passed earlier now faced them, his machine gun pointed at their bellies.

With her hands raised in the air, she looked over her shoulder. Everyone in the room was riveted to the front where Bez stood, a woman at his side, a gun to her head.

"I wanted to make sure you behaved, Lieutenant," Bez said loudly, trying to be heard over the crying and sniffling throughout the room. "Give me the box with the encryption key in it and I'll tell you where your brother is."

"Show me my brother and I'll give you the key." Rafe took a step toward Bez. Claire moved with him, hating the fact that they had no backup and a machine gun pointed at their back.

Rafe grabbed for her, but she sidestepped him and faced Bez, walking slowly toward him. "Why don't you let these people go so we can talk?"

Bez gave her a once-over. "What would you like to talk about?"

Claire could see his hold relaxing on the woman. She took another step closer. "Why don't you tell me what's so important about that key? Why risk so much to get it?"

"Because it's my destiny. I was always destined to lead." He pressed the gun to the woman's temple and she whimpered. "Give it to me. Now."

The woman stared at Claire, terror in her eyes. "Please give it to him. I don't want to die," she cried.

Claire could see her shaking with fear. "Stay calm." She put out her hand. "Bez, you can always tell a true leader by the way he treats those who are beneath him. You don't want to hurt these people, do you?"

"Do you have any idea who these people are?" Bez sneered. "They are western journalists, who lie and exploit people for money. They're all terrorists." He waved the gun toward the crowd and several people ducked. "You there." He pointed to a man sitting at a table near him who was one of the few still sitting straight in his chair. "You have a recording device?"

The man held up an iPhone. "Just this."

Bez waved him over. "I want you to record this. So people know who's in charge." He pulled the woman closer to him. She let out a little scream as the man got into position to record.

"Okay, it's recording." The man's hand shook, but other than that, he looked calm.

Bez pulled himself up to his full height as he looked directly at the iPhone. "I am the new amir. This is only the beginning."

Claire signaled to Rafe to go around the other side of Bez while he was distracted, but Bez looked in their direction and point his gun at Rafe. "Stop right there," he commanded, turning the gun back to the woman's head. "Stop or I'll kill her. It will be recorded for all the world to see and they will know I am to be feared. I—"

"Let these people go and I'll give you the key," Rafe offered.

Bez dropped his chin in incredulity to stare at them, his lips pursed in anger. "What about your brother? Which one would you save? These people or him?"

"Why does it have to be a choice?" Claire asked, trying to placate him. "You will be getting everything you want when you have that encryption key. Give us the lives of the people in this room and Vince Kelly."

At that moment, over the earpiece came a strange humming. Claire tilted her head trying to place it and when she did, her eyes went wide. "Ring around the rosy, a pocket full of posies . . ." she whispered along with the tune. Not even questioning where the humming was coming from she turned with her arms wide to warn the people directly behind her. "Bomb! Get down now!"

It was as if her words set off a chain reaction. People started to crawl under chairs and tables, screaming, as the explosion started in the far corner and the blast flew outward.

Claire threw down a table for cover from debris then pulled a woman frozen to her chair with fright under the table with her. Coughing and choking she knew they needed to get out before the fire got closer, but the room was in complete pandemonium. With a peek around the table corner she saw Rafe fighting with Bez, trying to get to his gun. Smoke obscured them, but she knew she had to get to Rafe. Crawling toward where she'd last seen him, while screaming into her mic for her father to get someone in the ballroom, she tensed when she heard gunshots—two tiny pops in the cacophony surrounding her, but that echoed in her earpiece. With a cry she stood and ran toward the sound, but another explosion rocked the ballroom, knocking her off her feet.

Water sprayed down from the ceiling sprinklers. Claire picked herself up off the floor she spotted Bez and his guard dragging Rafe toward the outside exit. Through her earpiece she could hear groaning and she prayed that was Rafe and he was still alive. "Check him for tracking devices." There was a crackle on the comms. "Take his boots off and get him in the car," came through loud and clear.

She tried to push through the crowd to get closer, but as soon as people saw the open door they rushed it and Claire lost sight of him. She joined the stream of people jammed against the tiny door opening like pressure building up behind a bullet. Claire might as well have been against a brick wall with the way people were packed together. Pressing her fingers against her earpiece so she could hear any sound that came over it, she was dismayed to hear Bez's voice once again. "He's wired. Get that off before we go."

She tried once more to get through the crowd, but there was no way. Without his tracker, his wire, or his mic, they were blind. She had to hope someone on the team had picked him up on the outside.

With eyes streaming from the smoke, Claire finally made it out of the ballroom after what seemed like an eternity. She bent over her knees, trying to catch her breath. When she straightened, her father was walking toward her, his face grim.

"Did you find Rafe? I heard gunshots and saw Bez and that guard dragging him out."

Her father's face said everything, but Claire needed to hear the words, her stomach plummeting as he touched her shoulder. "He's gone. Bez has him."

Chapter Fifteen

Claire used every bit of training she had to keep her in her seat, her hands clenched on the table in front of her. She wanted to be out there, looking for Rafe. Her father had been on the phone for the better part of the night trying to figure out what went wrong at the hotel. After listening to his side of the conversation, it didn't look good for Rafe.

Where is he? He'd been through so much in the last few days. How much more could he take?

The door opened and Commander Ludin walked through. He barely cast a glance in her direction, before moving to stand in the corner to wait for her father.

His demeanor bothered her. *How can he be so calm?* She shot to her feet. "Do you know anything about where Bez has taken Rafe? Any ideas where he could be?"

His gaze flicked in her direction, but he didn't say anything.

Anger rose in her and she struggled to control it. "I'm sorry, maybe you didn't hear me. Do you know where Rafe is? Have your people got anything that might help us?" Her voice was tight.

Ludin finally turned toward her. "No, I don't know where he is."

She narrowed her eyes. It was hard to keep her voice level, but she knew if she were going to get any information out of him at all, she had to fight to stay calm. "We're going to find him, so if you or anyone you know were involved, you should tell us now. We can still fix things, it hasn't gone too far yet." *I hope.* "I could put in a good word if you cooperate."

Ludin practically sneered and leaned against the wall. "Your word means nothing to me."

Is that a confession? Claire clenched her fists. "Our only concern is getting Rafe and Vince back safely. If you can help us, now is the time to speak up."

"The men are most likely dead by now. Bez isn't known for his kindness, especially to Americans." Ludin pushed off the wall and stood like a little Napoleon with his hand on his uniform. "Now if you'll excuse me, I need to talk to Chief Michaels."

Claire didn't move. There wasn't any way she was going to leave. If Ludin had information to share, she was going to hear it.

Her dad finally hung up the phone, letting out a deep breath as he sat down. "I could hardly hear with you two arguing. What do you have, Ludin?"

He motioned toward Claire. "I need to speak to you in private, Chief."

Skip immediately shook his head. "She can hear whatever you have to say."

"Chief, I'm afraid this is of a very sensitive nature. I must insist that it stay between us." Ludin stood at attention now, as if to remind them of their status as military colleagues.

Her father looked at her, the apology in his eyes plain to see. "Claire, can you give us a minute?"

Claire wanted to protest, to squeeze the information out of Ludin right then with her bare hands, but she merely nodded and left the room. She was proud of herself for not slamming the door.

She sat down at the same table Rafe had used just yesterday when he'd left the initial team meeting. Dropping her head in her hands, she closed her eyes. All she could see was Luke, kneeling, staring at the camera and the phone on her father's desk that kept ringing with updates that gave them hope of his safe return. Hopes that were raised for nothing.

This isn't like that. I can do something to change this outcome. She just had to think. *Maybe I should see if Sam's come up with anything on that file yet.*

"Is this seat taken, ma'am?"

Claire looked up to see Patrick standing in front of her. "No." She sat back in her chair while he joined her. "Have you heard anything?"

"About Rafe? No." He leaned on the table. "Have you?"

She shook her head. "Did you get checked out? That was a nasty bump you got."

"I can't believe Bez got the drop on me. I should have been there for Rafe." Patrick sat down. "And you. What are you doing out here all by yourself?"

"Ludin needed to talk to my father alone, so I came out here to get some fresh air." With a quick look around, she realized they were the only ones in the courtyard, the only sound the rattle of dishes as the cooks got breakfast ready for the base.

"Maybe you should eat something and lie down. You look like you're ready to drop."

Claire felt annoyed. *Why did everyone keep saying that?* "I'm okay. As soon as we get the next status update I will."

It was a tiny lie. She didn't have any intention of lying down. If she was there when something came in, maybe it would make the difference in bargaining for Rafe's life.

"How long have you known Rafe?" Patrick asked.

Claire watched him chew on his thumbnail. When she thought about it, he seemed nervous. "Not long. What about you?"

"About a year. We were stationed on the border of Pakistan and Afghanistan together. Being in a place that primitive bonds you, you know." He watched her over his thumb. "That's how I know he'll get out of this. Rafe can take care of himself."

"I'm sure he can." Claire relaxed her posture, realizing in a flash that Patrick could give her some information. "Were you with him for Eagle Claw?"

She instantly saw the wariness in his eyes. "Yeah. That was a tough mission. That's where this whole thing started."

"I know you captured Bez during that mission and that something went wrong." Claire gave him a small smile. "It was a hard mission for Rafe, especially after his injury, and getting sent home." She let her voice trail off. *Tell me, Patrick. Tell me the whole story.*

Patrick licked his lips, letting his hand fall into his lap. "Yeah, we got ambushed. They knew we were coming. The second we had Bez in our custody, the whole mountainside seemed to be crawling with insurgents coming toward us. Rafe managed to radio for immediate evac and then he was hit. He kept going, though, trying to get Bez to the helo. From my position I thought he was a goner, but Gary came along and took another way to the exit point even though he'd been wounded himself."

"So you weren't close then?"

"I was fighting my own battle." He gave her a tight smile that didn't quite reach his eyes. "Not all of us can be a hero like Rafe."

"Did all the team make it back safely?" She raised her eyebrows with the question. Patrick's nervousness had ratcheted up the longer they'd talked. *What is this about?* Her curiosity was piqued.

"Yeah, but Rafe and Gary were both injured. Gary was sent home immediately after because of the burns on his face, but Rafe stayed out for a couple of months, nursing his knee and trying to figure out what went wrong on that mission. He was obsessed over that."

"Did he ever find anything?"

"I don't know. You'll have to ask him." He seemed to realize what he'd said and quickly amended. "I mean, I know we'll get him back and then you can ask him." He put his elbows on the table, pushing closer to her. "You know, I really am a good listener if you want to talk. This must be hard on you."

Claire tapped her bottom lip with her finger. "Rafe never told you anything about his findings on that mission?"

Patrick leaned back, exasperation on his face. "You're not going to get obsessed over that, too, are you?"

Before Claire could answer, her father opened the office door. Ludin stepped out, looking angry as usual. "Claire could you come in here, please?" her dad asked.

She stood, part of her wanting to stay and see if she could get any more information out of Patrick. He was right about one thing, this all seemed to go back to Eagle Claw. But she wanted to know what her father had found out more. "I'm being summoned," she said to Patrick with a small smile. "I'll see you later."

He nodded and Claire could feel his eyes on her as she walked away. Picking up the pace, she reached her father's side and he stepped back so she could enter. "What did you find out?" It was impossible to keep the worry out of her voice.

Skip shut the door behind her. "We've got a problem, Claire."

"What?"

He went to the table and turned the laptop computer around. "Maybe you should sit down."

"Just tell me." She stood very still. "Dad, I hate being coddled. He's dead, isn't he?"

"No, no, it's not that. I'm sorry to make you think that." He ran a hand over his head. "It's all over the news. That recording from the ballroom has been broadcast worldwide." He turned it on and even with the shakiness of the recording it was clear enough to see

Bez talking about being the new amir and then the explosions ripping through the ballroom. Raising her eyebrows, she leaned forward. The guy had kept recording as Bez had fought with Rafe. The gunshots rang out, and even squinting at the footage, she still couldn't tell who'd been hit. The dark smoke hid everything she needed to know.

Claire felt weak with relief, her knees so rubbery she could barely keep herself upright. *He's still alive.* "Okay, so it's all over the news. Now what?"

"The president is scrambling to explain what's going on and as you can imagine, he's not thrilled to have to do that. He's sending in another team to take over." Her dad ran a hand over his face. "He thinks I'm too close to this after what happened to Luke."

"Are you?" She gave him a penetrating look.

"I don't know," he said with a shake of his head. "Maybe we both are. I didn't think I was." He sat down hard in his chair. "I think there's something else going on here."

Claire sat in the chair next to him. "What do you mean?"

"When we swept Vince's office, we found a Russian-made listening device in his phone. I figured that's how Bez found out Gary had decrypted the file because we know Vince called DoD for protection."

"That makes sense." She waited for him to continue. It was plain to see something was weighing heavily on him.

"We thought the bomb they used on Gary was a modified version of a prototype our defense department has been working on. But when the bomb experts got in on it, they found that only the outside looked like one of ours. The inside was Russian made. It had traces of the same explosives that were used in the Moscow Metro bombings. That's probably what they used today at the Intercontinental, since it's a specialty of Bez's and now we know it's not really ours."

"So they wanted it to look like our bomb? Why?"

"That's what I can't figure out. Did Bez want us to think he'd stolen our technology? Was it a show for the head of the cartel? And why did he use three bombs—on the roof, at the office, and at the house?"

Claire rubbed her eyes. "I don't know. What do we do now?"

"The president is calling us home as soon as the new team gets here."

That got her attention. "Home? But we've got to find Rafe."

"It's a direct order."

"He's your boss, not mine." The tears began to well.

"I'm your dad, Claire."

"I'm not going to do this again, Dad. I'm not going to wait for word and hope Rafe lives through it. I'm not going to another funeral of someone I care about, feeling like I should have done more—done better. I won't do it." A tear escaped and trickled down her cheek. She wiped it away, angry at her own weakness.

He patted her arm. "I know how you feel." They sat there in silence for a few minutes, each lost in their own thoughts. Her father finally spoke. "I have an idea, but if we do this, we have to be prepared for the consequences."

Claire rubbed the back of her neck, feeling the edge of her bandage, the physical consequences she'd already endured coming to mind. *I should probably change the bandage again. Rafe should change his, too.* It was doubtful Bez would care. "What's your idea?"

"Let's go after him ourselves. Even though Rafe's boots with the tracker were found in the bushes at the hotel, I have a few contacts in country and Bez was spotted heading toward the Paktika province. If he's trying to get into Pakistan, we could head him off. Patrick knows where his hideout was. He studied Bez along with the team while they prepared to capture him. We have as good a chance of anyone at finding him and I think timing is crucial. The sooner we go after him, the better. This new team is starting behind as it is and we could have the advantage."

Hope burned through Claire's chest. "What are we waiting for?"

"We have to do this carefully. Patrick might not come along. And we'll probably need Tom to give us some gear from the base." He turned back to his computer. "Ludin might also be beneficial. He could smooth the way with some Afghani contacts."

"I don't trust that guy."

"I'm not sure who to trust anymore." Her dad snapped his laptop shut. "We better get started if we're going to talk to Patrick, Tom, and Ludin get some gear and get out of here before the new team arrives."

"Are you sure you want to do this?"

Skip looked into her eyes for a long moment. "I don't want any family to have to go through what did, Claire. If there's something I can do to help, then I want to do it."

For just a second she was transported back to his office, to the fear and anxiety that gripped them as they waited for word of Luke. This time they weren't going to sit around, they were going to do something—together. "I agree. We can do this for Rafe. And for Luke." Even as she said the words she felt energy run through her veins. *Hold on, Rafe,* she thought. *Hold on a little longer.*

Chapter Sixteen

Rafe pulled his knees up to his chest to make himself as small as possible in the trunk so the bouncing wouldn't be as bruising. He gripped his upper arm, upsetting the delicate balance he was working for. He knew he needed to stop the bleeding from the new wound he'd acquired when Bez winged him. The explosion and shooting had been almost simultaneous and Rafe still didn't know which one had knocked him to the floor. He only knew that in a split second a plan had formed in his mind—if he faked unconsciousness Bez would abduct him and leave and Rafe would be able to keep the crowd left behind safe, including Claire. And maybe, if his luck held, Bez would take him to Vince and the potential for casualties would be down to one—him.

He reached down with his good hand to finger the outline of the small flash drive in his pocket, making sure it was still there. He was glad he'd given the eagle drive to Claire, but on a hunch he'd brought the drive shaped like a mole, just in case. It looked like he might need it now.

With another hard bounce, Rafe grabbed his arm once again. At least the new wound was on the same side as his burn, so his pain was still on just one part of his body. He hoped wherever they were going, they got there quickly.

Scrunched up in the trunk he worked on evening out his breathing and assessing how badly he was hurt by the level of pain he was experiencing. So far it looked like mostly his knee and his shoulder were the worst. The rest of his body was a dull ache in comparison to the stabbing agony in those two body parts. He tried to take his mind off of it by thinking about Claire. She had to be all right. He had to believe her father would have seen to that. Rafe had heard her scream his name and that had been the deciding factor in getting out of there. He wanted her safe. He wanted Vince safe, too, and if this was how it was going to happen then so be it. The car lurched around a corner and Rafe braced himself as best he could. *Please let me be going to my brother.*

He didn't have to wait long before the car stopped. Rafe steeled himself. The trunk popped open and a flashlight was shone in his face. Putting up his hands to mute the glare, the guard hauled him out of the trunk by the arm. As soon as Rafe had his legs under him, he shoved the guard off. "Watch it!" Grabbing his arm again, he could tell the wound had opened up again. Pulling on his sleeve, he used his teeth to tear off a strip. Quickly wrapping it around the bloody wound, he stepped forward, but the guard blocked his way.

"Stay here." The man's voice was so low it was barely more than a growl.

Rafe ignored him and took another step before hearing his knee pop. Suppressing a groan, he leaned against the car and looked down at his leg. The swelling was getting worse. He wiped a bead of sweat from his forehead. All he could hope for was that it would keep him upright and able to move when he needed it. He was too close to reaching his pain threshold.

Bez came around the corner of the car to face him. "Tie him up and search him," he commanded the guard, handing him some rope. The guard approached and Rafe dutifully held out his arms, wanting to make this as painless as possible. Thankfully the makeshift bandage was helping a bit. Bez stood silently and watched while the guard tied Rafe's hands in front of him, sweating profusely.

"Are you okay?" Rafe asked. "You're sweating a lot."

The guard grunted and did a double pull on each knot, making Rafe suck in a breath as the rope cut into his wrists. "Just making an observation."

With a swipe of his hands on his pants, the guard thoroughly frisked him. "Hey, watch it," Rafe protested as the pocketknife he'd hidden in an inner pocket was pulled out. With an eyebrow raise, the guard handed over the flash drive and the knife to Bez.

"You brought the flash drive with you," Bez said, one side of his mouth lifting into a strange half-smile.

His smile is as unbalanced as his mind, Rafe thought. "You have what you want, now take me to my brother," he shot back.

"When this is verified, then I will take you to your brother." Bez was staring at the flash drive in his hand, turning it over and over as if he was afraid it might disappear.

Finally he pocketed it and went around to the driver's side of the car. He stood there, looking at the sky.

"What are we waiting for?" Rafe asked, feeling strained to the limits. The rocky soil dug into Rafe's bare feet. What he wouldn't give for his boots right now!

"Our ride should be here shortly." As soon as Bez spoke, Rafe heard the hum of helicopter rotors. "It's a déjà vu, isn't it? The last time we were together, waiting for a helicopter, I was being taken away by your countrymen to suffer at their hands. Now the shoe is on the other foot so to speak and we will see what you can endure." He tilted his head and looked at Rafe's feet.

Rafe clenched his jaw. "Why don't you just tell me where my brother is and our business will be over. You go your way, I'll go mine."

The helicopter landed and Bez's guard took Rafe's arm. "I have a few plans for you as soon as the decryption is complete." Bez led the way toward the helicopter, only slowing down once to call over his shoulder. "I won't spoil the surprise."

Rafe winced with every step. His knee and probably his feet would never be the same. He looked back to see a small blood trail in the dirt behind him. He might have been happy to leave footprints if there had been any chance of someone finding them. Grinding his teeth together, he kept walking.

They finally made it to the helicopter and Rafe wasn't surprised when the guard pulled a hood from behind the seats and put it over his head. It was foul-smelling and Rafe almost gagged. He put his chin to his shoulder to push it aside. It was hard to breathe. "Hey, has your guard been wearing this? It smells a lot like him."

He got a smack on the back of his head, which almost caused him to fall. Not being able to use his hands was limiting, but at least they were tied in front of him, so he could keep some sort of balance.

Shoved into a seat, hooded and tied, Rafe tried to count the minutes the flight took them. If he had to guess, Bez would go back to the Paktika province where he had connections. But if Bez was planning to take him across the border to Pakistan, that would make things a lot harder for him. Patrick could possibly lead the team to Paktika and find him, but Bez could disappear with Rafe in Pakistan and no one would ever know what had happened to him.

He leaned his head back against the metal behind his seat, wishing that Gary were here. No, he wouldn't want him caught in this mess. He just wanted Gary alive. He always had the backup plans, had always had Rafe's back. The look of resignation on Gary's face just before he was killed rose in Rafe's mind. *If only I could have saved him!* Regret roiled in his belly.

The only person he could depend on now was Patrick. He hadn't known Patrick as long as Gary and he'd definitely been harder to get to know. Patrick was added to the team specifically for the mission to capture Bez and seemed to be good at intelligence analysis both on the field and off. But he kept to himself during the training, doing exactly what was asked of him and no more. It was frustrating sometimes because he couldn't get a read on Patrick and when the mission went south, Rafe instinctively knew he wouldn't help him get out of it.

Rafe hoped he would help him now—that he was able to help him. For a moment, back at the hotel, when Patrick hadn't answered Rafe thought that Bez might have him. Knowing now that Bez didn't, Rafe could only hope that Patrick hadn't been hurt in the explosion. *Or worse.*

The helicopter started to descend and Rafe sat up straight, still breathing through his mouth to deal with the smell. No one said a word as the helicopter powered down. He heard the door open and the air was as musty as the hood over his head. Someone yanked his arm and he got out, forced to follow wherever he was led. Cursing the hood, he twisted his head to see if he could get even a small glimpse of where they were, but the material was too heavy. He stubbed his toe on a rock and grunted, knowing he had to turn his concentration on getting to wherever they were going without being dragged along.

The guard stopped and gripped Rafe so he would stay where he was. They waited for a minute before Rafe heard a door open. The smell of smoke and something cooking greeted him. Maybe his nose was a bit sensitive, but whatever was cooking reeked worse than the hood on his head. They stepped over a threshold and the ground under his feet smoothed out. *Dirt floors.* Grateful for the reprieve on his battered feet and knee, Rafe walked alongside the guard, counting his steps and trying to listen for any sounds or clues as to where they might be. All was silent.

Finally Rafe was told to sit and the hood was taken away. He looked around. He was sitting on a chair in the middle of a small room, the lone candle burning in the corner casting shadows over the table on the opposite side of the room.

"Wait here." The guard parted a heavy curtain and stepped out into a hall. Before it flapped shut, Rafe caught a glimpse of Bez holding out the flash drive to another man. *Verifying the encryption key.*

Rafe stood and limped over to the curtain. He could only make out a few words. "Chapa. Two days." Bez's voice was getting further away.

Was Chapa coming here? Was Bez delivering product to Chapa in two days? The possibilities were endless and there were no answers. Rafe limp-hopped quickly back to his chair, hoping he hadn't left any blood drops behind to give away what he'd been doing. He sat down and bent over as the guard came in as if studying the ropes on his hands. "Can I get some water?"

The guard leaned against the table and said nothing.

"Okay, how about taking the ropes off my wrists? It's not like I can go anywhere." He held up his hands and hopefully raised his eyebrows.

Again, the guard just stared. Rafe gave up and tipped his head back. When he'd been stationed in Paktika, one of their duties had been to go house to house and check for anything suspicious, but the houses weren't like any back home. They were little compounds, with brown brick exterior rooms that surrounded a small courtyard area in the middle—sort of like an American fort from the Old West. The room he was currently in looked like every other one he'd checked when he was on active duty. But that didn't necessarily mean they were in Paktika. It gave Rafe some hope that they were, though, and that maybe Patrick could help find him.

Not wanting to rely on merely hoping someone would find him, Rafe knew he had to make a plan. If they really were going to take him to Vince, the first item of business was getting some shoes and a weapon. Then he would get Vince out of here. There had to be some way to contact the U.S. even if he had to go over the mountains to do it. He thought of the reflective tape stuck in his pocket. That might be their ticket home if they could get to a high enough point to be seen.

The curtain opened and Bez entered. "We can't open the key. What fingerprint does it need?"

Rafe shook his head in disgust. "It needs Gary's fingerprint. But you took care of that, didn't you?"

Bez stood over him. "There is always a back way for programs like these. I know how you people work. Tell me the way to access it since Gary's fingerprint is not available."

"If there is a back door, we weren't able to find it," Rafe lied. "Gary was the only one with the answers. That's why they had Gary working on the decryption in the first place, because he was smart enough to figure it out. But you weren't smart enough to keep him around."

Bez pulled back his arm and Rafe lifted his chin, knowing what he intended to do and wanting Bez to know he wasn't afraid of him. His head snapped back as Bez's fist connected with his jaw, but Rafe absorbed the pain, feeling the surge of adrenaline rush through his veins. *This is for you, Gary.* He stood up, eye-to-eye with Bez. "That's all you've got?" He tasted the blood in his mouth and spit it at Bez's feet. "What a coward. Untie my hands and fight me like a man."

Bez shoved him backward into his chair and hit him again. "Tell me how to unlock the key." Bez rubbed his knuckles and glared down at Rafe.

"You killed the only man who knew how to do it," Rafe said. He kicked out his legs, hitting Bez with all the strength he had left. Bez fell flat on his back, but his guard was on Rafe before he could feel any satisfaction. His blows were harder than Bez's and Rafe was dizzy, barely able to breathe. He couldn't take much more.

"Enough," Bez said finally. "Maybe you'll tell me if your brother is here with a gun to his head."

The image rose in Rafe's head at the same speed as the bile in his throat. "I told you, no one but Gary knows." The words sounded garbled to him, one side of his jaw as numb as when he'd been to the dentist. *I'll probably need a dentist pretty soon.* He licked the corner of his lip. "I kept my end of the deal and I expect you to keep yours. Where's my brother?"

Bez's eyes narrowed. "You've given me nothing. The key is useless."

"That's your fault, not mine," Rafe snapped.

"You want to be taken to your brother? Fine. I'm happy to do that." He nodded to his guard. "Let's go."

The guard took the hood off the table and put it back on Rafe's head. This time Rafe didn't even care about the smell. All he knew was they were taking him to Vince. Nothing mattered more than that—not the pain in his body or what he'd been through to get to this point. He was going to his brother.

Rafe was led by the arm back to what felt like another threshold, or maybe it was the same one they'd come in on, but it was the last smooth steps Rafe took. The ground was rocky again, cutting his feet, the pain numbing Rafe's ability to feel or think. His arm, his shoulder, his knee, his feet, his head, they all overwhelmed his senses, the pain beyond anything he'd ever felt before.

He tried to keep up, but he ended up stumbling along for what seemed like a good half mile. His feet felt slick and he had a hard time getting a foothold, even on the level ground. Rafe gritted his teeth together and put one foot in front of the other. *I'm going to Vince,* he repeated to himself over and over, trying to keep his thoughts in rhythm with his footsteps. *I'm going to Vince.*

The pain became almost unbearable and Rafe could feel blackness surrounding him—the edge of unconsciousness. He couldn't take anymore and stay lucid. He was about to drop when he was shoved into a car. Grateful to be able to rest a moment, he bent over and tried not to retch. *Breathe.*

After what felt like a few seconds, Rafe was pulled out of the car and marched a few feet away. The hood was finally taken off and he was standing in front of a hole in the ground. A very dark hole. "You put Vince in there?" Rafe asked incredulously, his throat so dry it made his voice hoarse. "Is he still alive?"

"You're about to find out," Bez said as he pushed Rafe toward the hole. Bez's guard grabbed Rafe's arms and forced him over the dark hole, holding him suspended in the air. The ropes cut into Rafe's wrists, but he held on, the guard the only thing keeping him from falling into the pit. If he let go, he couldn't tell how far the fall would be. The guard slowly lowered him down until his arm couldn't stretch anymore. A draft came up from the blackness and Rafe shivered. *Please let Vince still be alive.*

And then he was falling.

Chapter Seventeen

Claire looked over the barren and rocky landscape. It had taken longer than she'd thought for Tom to get them a ride to the outpost near where they'd captured Bez before. But they hadn't gone to the camp. Instead, Ludin had insisted the rest of the team stay at a property he owned nearby. He had been whispering furiously to her father the entire trip. Claire was anxious to know what was going on, but they hadn't had a moment alone. *Why aren't we going to the base?*

They bounced over the rough terrain until they finally stopped in front of a small compound. The brick was the same color as the soil and the building blended into the landscape. As soon as she was over the threshold, however, she felt the temperature drop a few degrees. It was a welcome respite. "Is this your home, Ludin?"

"It is my sister's home," he said abruptly. He clenched his hands as they went into the house, his boots almost grinding into the smooth wood floor. Claire followed behind him, his back so tense she could almost see his shoulder muscles straining as he marched forward. He led them to a back room where a younger man was sitting at a table. He stood when Ludin entered and the two men greeted each other with a hug. Claire was curious, watching the younger man who was as tall as Ludin, but didn't look at all like him. *They're definitely not brothers.*

Ludin spoke with him quietly in their native tongue before he turned back to the group he'd brought in with him. "This is my brother-in-law Hadir." Ludin's introduction was as abrupt as his personality. "We'll want to use the house as a base of operations."

"As an honor to Fatima?" Hadir's looked down as he spoke. Claire was surprised he knew English.

"Yes," Ludin agreed, his expression darkening to the familiar scowl.

Hadir bowed slightly. "Welcome to my home." His English was slow, but clear.

Claire wrinkled her brow. *How was this an honor to Fatima? Where was she?* "Thank you for your hospitality. Is Fatima your wife? I'd like that thank her personally."

Hadir shook his head. "I'm sorry, but that's not possible." He motioned them toward the hall. "There are rooms this way you can use. Follow me."

Claire felt embarrassed. She wasn't used to this culture and felt she'd stepped on toes somehow. She glanced at her father. He lifted a shoulder, as if to say 'let it go,' but he kept his hand at her back as they walked down the hall as a show of support. Ludin kept looking back at them as if he was afraid they were going to turn and run. "What's going on, Dad? What's Ludin so chatty about and why aren't we at the base? That would make more sense."

"Ludin has a hunch, but I still don't know if I can go along with it. Yet," he whispered to her.

"What kind of hunch?"

"I can't say right now." He looked behind them at Sam and Patrick. Sam was trying to catch up, his laptop bag slapping against his thigh as he moved.

Claire nodded. She would have to be patient. Hadir stopped and motioned for them to continue into the room to his left. It had a

Julie Coulter Bellon

computer in one corner and a sophisticated-looking communications system next to it with tables and benches around the perimeter.

"Do you think we'll be able to do all the work from here?" Skip asked.

"Yes." Ludin sat down at the small chair and booted up the computer. "Everything we need is here."

Sam pushed his way into the room. "I'm sure *I'll* be able to let you know if this is adequate or not." He took out his laptop. "We should get set up. If Rafe is still alive we're going to need this encryption key and I'm the only hope this team has in getting a bargaining chip for him."

Claire wanted to roll her eyes. "Rafe's still alive, Sam. We can't afford to think otherwise." Sam shrugged, then bent his head and started to boot up his computer. *He's alive, he's alive.* She repeated the phrase over and over to herself like she had since she'd first heard the shots. *He has to be alive.* She pushed away the images of her brother's outcome.

Patrick walked over to her and put his hand on her shoulder. "I'm here if you need me." He bent to look at her, his red-rimmed eyes mirroring her own. Neither of them had slept in so long. "I've got a great ear for listening that's available anytime you want it."

Claire gave him a small smile. "Thanks, Patrick." In a profession that was mostly made up of men, she'd seen that look before. He wanted more than she was willing to give. With an inward sigh, she hoped she'd read the situation wrong. *Maybe he's just trying to be nice.* He stood there awkwardly as if expecting her to start talking to him right that minute. The smile felt frozen on her face so she finally turned to her father. "What can I do to help?"

"I had Captain Reed send over the recording of Gary's hostage situation. We also have the footage from the hotel. I want you to listen to the tapes and watch that footage. There has to be

169

something we're missing. Maybe you can see something we haven't that will give us a clue here."

Claire's stomach sank. Going over those tapes. Knowing how it ended. "Okay," she said, not meeting her father's gaze. She rolled her shoulders. *Stay professional.*

"Ludin already has some feelers out with his contacts for any unusual activity around Bez's known locations."

Claire snapped to attention at that news. The security Ludin had said was solid at the hotel had resulted in this whole situation in the first place. "Are you sure?" she said, keeping her voice low so only her father could hear.

"Yes," he said, looking her in the eye. "I need you to listen to those tapes and then coordinate anything you get with Patrick."

They both looked over at Patrick who was talking with Sam, leaning over him, getting in his space. It was obvious that Sam was upset with someone looking over his shoulder. "Just leave me alone and let me work," Sam said, waving angrily at Patrick.

Claire walked over to where the two men were, picking up the other laptop. "Why don't you and I work on the other table?" she suggested to Patrick. Sam sent her a grateful look. Patrick silently agreed and together they walked over to the table on the opposite side of the room. He began setting out maps, putting them down a little harder than necessary.

"Are you going to make a grid?" Claire tried to catch his eye as he stared holes into Sam's back. "Do you have an idea of where to start?"

He turned his attention to Claire finally, absently touching one sleeve. "I think we should start with the place Bez used to store his heroin. It's well-guarded and large enough to be a base of operations for whatever Bez is planning and he knows it well. He would be comfortable there." He looked down at the map. "Although if he's running scared, he might go back to his cave hideouts."

"Where are those?"

Patrick motioned to several marked spots on the map. "He had several. That's why capturing him was such a difficult mission. There were so many chances for him to get away and we really have no idea how extensive the cave system is." He stood shoulder to shoulder with Claire. "But we got him then and we'll get him this time."

Slipping his arm around her, he gave her a quick squeeze. *Please don't go there.* His arm felt heavy and awkward and Claire politely stepped away, not wanting to hurt his feelings. "Thanks." She opened the laptop, quickly booting it up to give her hands something to do. "I'm supposed to be looking for clues from when Bez took Gary hostage." Patrick's eyes widened. "Sorry. I'll put headphones on." She reached into the case and took out the headphones.

"It just caught me off-guard, that's all. Gary was a great guy. I can't believe he's dead. Was it really a Black Widow bomb?"

Claire plugged in the headphones and sat down. "Yeah, it was. I really am sorry." She looked up at Patrick and for just a second, she thought he looked like he was going to cry. She felt horrible. "Like you said, you got Bez once, you'll get him again. He'll answer for what he's done."

She waited for the MP3 files to load, watching Patrick as he went back to the maps. He seemed rattled, knocking over a pile of maps, flicking quick glances in her direction. Glad for the headphones so he didn't have to listen to Gary, she put them on. Hearing the familiar voices of Captain Reed, Colby, and Bart made her homesick. She could really use them about now, both professionally and personally.

Rafe's voice came through loud and clear as she talked with Gary, trying to figure out the texts. He was talking about this being someone they knew in the military because of the rhyme. "It's no coincidence," he said. Claire leaned forward and put her elbows on the table. How would Bez have known that rhyme? They'd heard it at the hotel as well, right before the explosion. *Ring around the rosy, a pocketful of posies* had been hummed into her earpiece.

Claire bit her lip as the tape went on, Rafe telling her to get back. Bez had wanted her to take off her Kevlar and put on the bomb vest. She'd considered it for a moment, but from the look on Rafe's face, she wouldn't have gotten the first Velcro strap undone. The thought made her smile. He was so worried about everyone around him. Remembering the last glimpse of his unconscious body being dragged away took the smile from her face. *He's alive. Think of the best case scenario.*

She listened to the negotiation all the way through to the end, hearing Gary's last warning. "Don't trust anyone and remember Eagle Claw." Was he trying to tell them it was Bez, since that mission had been about capturing Bez? Or was it something else? Who didn't he want them to trust? She took the earphones out, cracking her thumb knuckles. It was getting harder and harder to resist closing her eyes, but she knew she wouldn't be able to sleep until they had something to go on—an idea of where Rafe might have been taken.

Where would Bez take hostages? The tapes made it clear he liked to play games with his victims. Would he go to a compound or a cave? Her instinct told her he would want to hunker down, but after being detained he would want some comforts. If that were true, he would go to the compound. She went round and round in her head with no clear answers. Usually her gut gave her a direction, but right now she had nothing.

Rubbing her fingers in circles over her temples, she realized he might just be holing up as well, trying to decide what to do with his hostages. Then the cave would make more sense. But if he'd planned this as carefully as he claimed, then he would know what he was going to do with the hostages. The image of her brother's closed casket popped into her head and she knew she didn't ever want to be in that situation again. Especially not with Rafe.

She looked up at her father who was still whisper-arguing with Ludin in the corner. Her father seemed truly angry. *What is going on?*

Before she could get up and go over, Patrick blocked her way. "Figure anything out?"

Claire pressed her lips together. He was starting to irritate her with all his hovering. "How many people knew about that little rhyme the SEAL team said before a munition went off?" she asked him.

"I don't know, just the team I guess. Maybe someone could have heard the guys talk about it." Patrick backed up a step. "Why?"

"How would Bez know about it?"

"He wouldn't."

Claire filed that away. Maybe Gary had mentioned it to someone while Bez bugged the offices. And Vince had known about it from Rafe. "I know that Bez likes to play games. And he's planned this. After being in U.S. custody, I think he's going to want to go somewhere he'd feel safe."

"Well, your gut is in agreement with mine." He smiled and held out his hand to help her up. "I think we should try the compound first, but it's going to take some planning. Should we go tell your father?"

She closed the laptop and stood, pretending not to notice his hand, her annoyance level running high. He held it in the air a second longer and she saw a tremor run through it. "Are you okay?"

Patrick closed his fist. "I'm fine. Is everything okay with you? You seem like you're avoiding me all of the sudden."

Claire winced inside. *I really don't want to have this conversation right now.* "No, not avoiding you. Just trying to concentrate on finding Rafe, that's all."

"Those tapes were hard for you to listen to, weren't they?" Patrick fell into step beside her as she headed toward her father.

"Yes. I wish things had turned out differently for Gary that day." She could hardly concentrate on the conversation. As soon as Ludin saw them approaching, he stopped talking and stared at her. Every instinct she had was telling her he was hiding something. But why wouldn't her dad let the team in on it?

Her father turned to face them. "Have you got something?"

"Sir, we're in agreement that we think Bez would take Rafe to a compound he used to store heroin." Patrick unrolled the map. "It's here. But it's also guarded so we're going to have to figure out how to get around that."

Skip took the map from him and walked over to the table. "Tell me what you know."

Claire stayed where she was in the background, watching them. Patrick was bouncing his foot as if he couldn't wait to get out of there. *He's eager.* And then Ludin was standing in the corner, his arms folded, watching them all. *What is really going on here?*

Her father motioned for Ludin to come over and Patrick stepped back when Ludin reached his side. Running a hand over his face, Patrick arched his neck. He looked as tired as Claire felt. He glanced at her, then he moved to the door and stepped out. Claire followed.

He walked down the hall and went directly to the front door. Claire was surprised to see him leaving the compound. She stayed out of sight as he got into the Jeep they'd left on the side of the house. *Is he going to leave us here?*

He sat in the driver's seat, his head over the wheel, looking depressed. It made Claire feel guilty about brushing him off earlier.

Deciding to assuage her conscience and find out what was going on with him, she stepped out and approached the Jeep. Going

174

around to the passenger side, she opened the door and got in, but left the door open. "Is everything okay? You look a little pale."

He didn't lift his head off the wheel, just turned his face to look at her. "Just worried is all."

"Worried about finding Rafe?"

"That, and other things." He finally lifted himself off the wheel and tilted his head back to look at the ceiling. "You know, I feel like I've given my life to the military. All of it. And there's nothing left for me."

"It's tough to have a personal life when you're in the service," Claire agreed. Hot wind was blowing in behind her so Claire closed the door. "What brought this up?"

He gave her a probing look. "You love your job, though, right? Even though it robs you of a personal life?"

"Yeah, I do. There's a lot of satisfaction in following clues, solving cases. Especially getting a hostage out safely."

"Do you think Rafe even has a chance?"

Claire thought back to the first time she'd seen Rafe kneeling on that roof, the calm expression he had on his face, even though he'd had a gun to his head. "Yes, I do. He just seems like the kind of guy that's ready for anything."

"You sound like you know him pretty well."

Surprised at the frustrated tone in his voice, Claire backed off a bit. *What's going on?* "Like I said, he was a hostage the first time I met him. And right after, his brother was taken. There hasn't really been time to get to know him. But I have seen hostages before and if anyone can survive this, Rafe can."

"But that's why you don't want to get to know me, because you want to get to know him." Patrick turned in his seat then, leaning toward her. He was too close, but Claire didn't back up and held her ground. She was used to guys trying to intimidate her. It was time to set some boundaries.

"I don't know what you're implying, Patrick. We're here on a case to get Rafe and his brother home safely. I'm not here for a relationship." She kept her voice low, but firm.

He backed off, taking a deep breath. "I'm sorry. I think this whole thing just got to me." With a tilt of his head, he grimaced at her. "It's just hard to cope with being alone sometimes. It seems like everyone around me is dead or dying."

"Rafe's not dead. No one has to die here if we play our cards right." She reached out to touch his arm. "We can do this. We can save Rafe and Vince."

Patrick looked down at her hand on his arm before he leaned over and locked her door. "No, we can't."

She should have recognized something was off. She'd looked at hostage-takers before, but all she could do was stare at the gun now pointed at her. He started the car with his other hand.

"Don't do this."

"It's too late, Claire. I don't want to bring you to him. I really don't. But I have to. Please know I'm really sorry."

Chapter Eighteen

Rafe felt like a million knives were stabbing him in the head and shoulder. Trying to open his eyes made the pain worse, but he did it anyway. The light that greeted him almost put him over the edge. Last night came rushing back to him. He'd passed out in the cave.

"Vince?" he called out, his voice little more than a croak. He was so thirsty.

His head and shoulder protested vigorously as he tried to sit up. What he really wanted to do was lie back down, but he had to find Vince. He groaned, realizing his hands were still tied. As best he could, he bumped his arms against the walls to leverage the shoulder that didn't feel like it was on fire against the stone so he could get his bearings. The pain was excruciating. When he was settled, he took a deep breath and closed his eyes. *I can do this.*

He began to work on getting his hands free of the ropes that still tied them. Using his teeth, he pulled the knots until his jaw ached. It took a little while, but he finally got free. Rubbing his now sore jaw, with his already sore hand, he looked around the small room, the light from the hole above not helping to illuminate the corners of the cave. He couldn't see anyone or anything except some flour-looking type sacks against one end. With every ounce of effort he could muster, he called out again. "Vince?"

A small moan came from behind the sacks and Rafe pulled himself up as quickly as he could to limp over to where it had come from. With a glance down at his knee, he could see why he couldn't put any weight on it. It had swollen to the size of a football. Every movement was like stepping on razor blades and running them up his leg. It was probably the worst physical pain he'd ever felt in his life, but nothing prepared him for the sight of his brother lying behind two large sacks, his face bruised almost beyond recognition. *I'm going to kill Bez.*

Rafe sank down next to him, grateful to be off his feet. He didn't dare touch his brother, since every inch of him was black and blue. "Vince, it's Rafe."

Vince tried to open one swollen eye. "Rafe?" He coughed and gasped for breath.

It was hard not to reach out to him. "I'm going to get you out of here." If it was the last thing he did.

"Can you walk?"

"Yeah, I think I can walk." He squinted his eye that still opened at his brother. "You look terrible. Worse than usual."

At that, Rafe laughed. Trust Vince to be concerned about looks at a time like this. "Well, you don't look that great yourself."

Vince gave him a lop-sided smile through his cracked and swollen lips. "Still look better than you. Always have, always will."

Rafe leaned over and gave his little brother a side hug with his good arm. "I wish I had a mirror right now little brother."

Vince reached to hug him back, but moaned as he moved. "I'm so glad you're here, but I think I've got a broken rib."

"Take it easy," Rafe admonished. "Looks like you took a beating."

"Yeah, they thought I knew something about what Gary was working on." Vince gingerly touched his ribs on his right side. "It hurts to breathe so I'm sure something's bruised, if not broken."

"Anything else?"

"Pretty much my entire body hurts right now. Except maybe my pinky toe. That's still good. What about you?" He nodded in Rafe's direction. "You look like you've been through a war. Well, more of a war than usual anyway."

"Three tours so far. And a little detour to get you." He pointed to his knee. "My knee's pretty bad. I don't know if I can walk. And I have a shoulder burn from the bombing that feels like the fires of Hades has set up camp there."

Vince's good eye widened. "What bombing?" He touched his jawline where the biggest bruise was on his face, stretching all the way to his cheek.

"The house. Bez bombed the house."

"Our house was bombed? Seriously? Mom and Dad weren't home yet were they?"

"No, no one was home. I was just going into the house when it blew."

"I can't believe this is all about that file Gary decrypted."

Rafe moved Vince's hands away so he could take a look at the bruises himself, turning his face toward the small amount of light they had. "I think you'll live. Let me look at your ribs." He felt his brother's torso. At least two ribs felt out of place. "Definitely broken." He pulled back so he could look Vince in the face. "What do you know about that file that was decrypted? Did the government even tell you how big this was?"

Vince's shoulders slumped. "I knew it was big, but I thought we could handle it. We kept it quiet, just like the DoD wanted. When Gary decrypted it, he said that we needed extra protection ASAP until we could get it back to them. I ordered it that morning and, well, you know what happened next."

"But Gary didn't tell you what was on it?" Rafe wanted to know how much Vince knew and what he could have said to Bez. *Does he know about the back door fingerprint?*

"No, he didn't. He wanted to wait until the DoD got there so he could tell us all at once. When I looked at the program he'd created to decrypt it, though, I knew it was going to revolutionize the company, triple our profits and help law enforcement all over the country. That's all I was thinking about."

That was the Vince he knew, always thinking of the bottom line. "Vince, we've got to figure out a way to escape."

Vince pointed to the hole in the ceiling. "That's how the guards come down and it's the only way in or out that I've seen." He brought his arm down and rubbed his wrists, which made Rafe rub his as well.

Rafe looked at his brother. He looked like he'd zoned out, thinking about the times those guards had come down and beat him. "I'm not going to let them hurt you again, Vince."

"I'm fine," Vince said, but Rafe wasn't convinced. It would be just like Vince to try and be strong for his brother, even as badly as he was hurting.

"Well, maybe if I put you on my shoulders you can pull yourself out."

"I'm not leaving you here," Vince said. "I say we stick together."

"We can't both get out of here and one of us needs to go for help. We need more than just the two of us."

"What about that rope over there? Is that from you?"

Rafe nodded.

"What if I go up first, then turn around and pull you up with the rope?"

Rafe shook his head. "With your rib injury, that's going to be hard. Not to mention the fact that I won't get far anyway on this knee. You just need to go and get some help to come back for me."

"How am I going to stand on your shoulders if one of them is burned? That could just injure you further," Vince pointed to what was left of Rafe's shirtsleeve. "And from the wound on your arm, it looks like you were shot as well." He shook his head. "Is there anything that hasn't happened to you?"

"Shut up. I can do it if you can," Rafe replied. *What's a little more pain?* His body was one big ball of pain right now, so having someone stand on him for a minute so they could escape didn't sound so bad if it meant them getting out of there.

Vince took a deep breath. "Okay, let's try it."

Rafe held up his hand. "When you get out, you need to go right to the mountains. Stay close to the rocks so you have a place to hide." He opened up a small Velcro pocket on his pants and ripped off a piece of tape. "This is a special reflective tape. It can help the U.S. find you. Just get to the highest point you can. They monitor those mountain ranges pretty closely."

Vince took the tape from him and put it on his shoulder. "Okay. Ready." He stood up, holding his side with one hand. They limped to the wall for support. "As soon as I'm on your shoulders, you just have to take about seven steps until I'm directly under the hole." He looked at Rafe. "Are you sure about this?"

"Yes," Rafe gritted out. He leaned over and cupped his hands. "I'm going to boost you."

Vince put his foot in Rafe's hands. "On the count of three. 1, 2, 3."

Rafe grunted as Vince's weight hit his hands. "Been having a few too many company lunches, Vince?"

"I'm going for the shoulders." Vince let his comment slide as he tried to balance in Rafe's hands. "Ready?"

No, Rafe wanted to say, but he nodded instead. Bracing himself, he tried to think of anything other than his brother's body standing on his burned shoulder with the trail of a bullet just below it. He stood as still as he could as Vince put his weight on him and couldn't hold back the cry that escaped from his lips.

Vince jumped down immediately.

"What are you doing?" Rafe said angrily as he bent over, gasping for breath. "I'm fine."

"No, you're not. And besides it wasn't enough. I needed another three feet at least."

Rafe couldn't hold himself up any longer. His knee and shoulder felt like a white hot poker had been stabbed into them. He didn't have anything left and sat down. "Got any other ideas?"

"Not really." Vince sat down next to him, rubbing a hand over his face. "I never thought I'd be in Afghanistan with you."

"Yeah, this is one place where I never imagined you'd ever be. Since you hate getting dirty and all."

Vince grimaced and brushed at his torn suit pants as if to prove Rafe's point. "I can't say I've ever been this dirty." He pulled his knees up slowly and let his hands hang over them. "Do you think anyone will find us?"

Should I be honest about their prospects? "I don't know," he said, finally "But I'm not ready to just lay down and die." What else could he do? It was his baby brother. "We've just got to give ourselves a minute to come up with another plan, that's all."

Vince started to say something else, but Rafe held up his hand. "Do you hear that?"

Voices were coming toward them. Familiar voices. *No*, Rafe thought. *Please, no.* He looked up at the hole. "Claire?"

"Rafe?" She sounded relieved. Within moments she was on her hands and knees, peering at him in the hole. At least she didn't look hurt.

Patrick's face appeared beside Claire's and he had a rope in his hands. "How far down are you?"

"I don't know, just throw the rope. Vince is hurt." Rafe's hopes soared. Maybe they'd get out of this after all. "Where's Skip? We're going to need some help. Bez is at a compound not far away."

"My dad's not coming," Claire said, her voice shaking a bit. "Patrick . . ."

"Patrick is working for me," Bez said triumphantly, stepping into view next to Claire. He pulled Claire back out of Rafe's line of sight.

"Claire!" Rafe shouted. "Bez, what's going on?" He clenched his fists when he didn't get an answer. "Don't hurt her."

Bez reappeared with Claire. She had a rope tied around her waist, taking a tentative step to the edge.

Rafe ground his teeth. *This is a nightmare.* He turned his focus to Claire and getting her down safely, reaching out for her as she swung on the rope. *Could this get any worse?* When she was beside him, she reached out to hug him, but even her light touch sent tremors of pain through him. It was worth it to feel her against him, though. "Claire," he murmured.

He looked up at Patrick and Bez. There had to be some other explanation than the one Bez was giving him. But what? "There's no way Patrick would ever work for someone like you, Bez."

Patrick stood over the hole, watching them. "I can explain, Rafe."

Before he could get another word out, Bez shoved him through the hole and Patrick landed with a thud at Rafe's feet with a yelp of pain.

"Now you'll have plenty of time to explain." Bez threw the rope in and walked away. "I'll be back."

Rafe got down in Patrick's face. *Traitor!* "We're here because of you? We may not get out of this. You better have something to say for yourself." Rage pulsed through him and he had to fight the urge to punch Patrick.

"I'd do anything to make it right, Rafe. Anything. You have to believe me. Let me explain. Please." Patrick was rolled into a ball at Rafe's feet and he was holding his lower leg in his hands.

Rafe straightened, every muscle in his body tense, and felt Claire right behind him. Strangely, her presence calmed him a bit. He took a breath. "I'm listening. And it better be good."

Chapter Nineteen

The first aid kit had been right behind her seat in the Jeep and Claire regretted not grabbing it. Rafe and Vince both looked like they were in pretty bad shape. At least Vince could still walk. Sort of. Rafe was barely able to stand. From the look of things, his knee was misshapen it was so swollen. His focus on Patrick might be the only thing keeping him upright.

"Being in Paktika was hard for me, Rafe. I never thought I'd see the things I've seen here." He sat up, not relinquishing his grip on his leg, but looking up at Rafe. "Some of the guys seemed to be coping better, and when I talked to a couple of them, they hooked me up with what they were using." He wiped the sweat away from his forehead. "I thought I could control it, but I couldn't. Pretty soon, I was running deals so I could get more. We were so far away from civilization I didn't think it would hurt anyone."

Claire stared at him. How could she have not seen the signs of a junkie? The red-rimmed eyes, the insomnia, the jittery movements. It was so clear now. "How long have you been using?"

"I've tried to stop so many times." He groaned and clutched his leg closer to him. "I think I broke my leg."

Rafe backed up a step, his fists clenched so tight his knuckles were white. "You betrayed your country, the SEAL team, everything you stood for. For what? So you could get high? Are you kidding me?"

Claire stood next to him. "Were you the one that told Bez about the *Ring Around the Rosy* rhyme? When was your first contact with him?"

"I didn't have any contact with him until today. There was a runner that would tell me what information I needed to give and when it was verified, then I got more heroin. There was always a go-between."

"So you're the reason Eagle Claw went south. The insurgents knew we were coming."

"That was the first time they'd wanted information on a mission. I figured if they just knew the day, we'd still have some element of surprise since they didn't know what time of day we were coming." The sweat was practically pouring off him now. "I knew we could still get through it." Patrick's voice was pleading. "And we did."

"But it nearly killed both Gary and me. We were never the same after that." Rafe turned his back on Patrick and faced the wall, his head tilted upward as if appealing to a higher power to help him process this. "Why didn't you say something to someone? Get some help instead of helping the enemy!"

Patrick awkwardly stood on one leg, hopping over to the wall near Rafe. "I was on a tight leash. They knew what they were doing. And I wasn't the only one. A lot of the guys in Paktika are doing heroin to deal with things out here." Patrick shook his head when Rafe didn't turn around. "You hold everyone to your standards because you're Mr. Perfect. You have no idea what it was like after you left. You were back home in the States living the good life with your rich family."

Rafe whirled around. "This has nothing to do with me. You gave away classified information and nearly got our team killed because of *your* choices. Let's get that straight." He limped over to stand in front of Patrick. "I might not be able to go back to active duty because of my knee because you couldn't cope. Not to mention Gary endured months of operations on his burns because *you couldn't cope!*" Rafe enunciated the last three words, practically yelling them in Patrick's face. "Don't tell me this is all about my standards and me being sent home so I don't know what it's been like out here. This is all about you, Patrick."

The men were practically nose-to-nose. They needed a buffer and Claire went to stand between them. "Let's stay calm," she said.

With a glance in her direction, Patrick looked down. "I'm sorry. And I'm sorry I brought you into this mess, Claire. I know I need help. I hate this."

He sounded pitiful, but after being so defensive with Rafe, Claire knew Patrick had a long ways to go in recovery. Claire tried to drum up some pity for him, but gave up. The man she was most worried about was Rafe. He looked so hurt and angry, and that only intensified when she took into account how bruised and broken his body was—how much he'd sacrificed for his country and his family. She reached out and lightly touched the middle of Rafe's back, hoping she hadn't hurt him. "Maybe we should talk about this when we're all out of here."

"Did you see anything on the way in? Does anyone know where we are?" Rafe ran a hand over his face.

"No, it was pretty barren. And Patrick told my dad to go to the compound, so I don't know that he'll look for the caves first." She touched his back again, hoping to offer a small amount of comfort.

Rafe finally turned to face her. She cringed when she saw his face full-on. So many bruises.

"You're hurt worse than I thought," she said, reaching up to touch his jaw. Out of the corner of her eye she saw Patrick turn away, retreating to a corner. The tension in the room eased a bit when the men were separated and Claire was relieved.

"I had a little fight with Bez, but he had a bit of an advantage." Rafe gave her a half-smile that quickly disappeared. "I'm worried you're not going to get out of this. You shouldn't be here."

Claire ran her thumbs over his wrists, the cuts and abrasion that ringed them telling her he'd been tied up. Tight. "We'll figure things out. I'm more worried about you and Vince needing a doctor."

Rafe shook his head. "I'm okay, and I think Vince will live." He glanced over at Vince who was watching them. He took her hand and led her over to him. "Claire, I'd like you to meet my brother Vince."

Claire smiled. "We've met actually. That day at Axis. Vince was pretty worried about you."

"I still am," Vince said. "We need to get him to a hospital."

Claire looked up at the hole in the ceiling. "I was just telling your brother that even if we did get out, there's not much around here. I didn't even see a building for miles."

"Well, we can't just sit here and wait for Bez to come back and kill us." Rafe looked over at Patrick leaning awkwardly on one leg in the corner. "Do you know what his plans are?"

"No. I'm not in his inner circle or anything." Patrick sat down, still holding one knee. "If I knew a way out, I would tell you."

Claire didn't know whether to believe him. He was an addict who needed help. She turned back to Rafe. "My father won't stop looking for us."

"I think we're on a limited time schedule. I heard Bez talking and he said Chapa and two days. I don't know what it means exactly, but whatever is happening is going to happen in two days." Rafe rolled his neck but the motion was guarded. It was as if he wanted to get a kink out, but it hurt to move. He slowly lowered himself to the ground. "Why do you think he put us all down here together? What do you think the game plan is?"

"I was wondering that myself. Although it would make it easier to kill us all if we're in one spot."

"I gave him a flash drive that he's trying to verify. I don't think he's going to be very happy when he realizes it isn't the one he wants."

"Buys us a little time. He won't want to kill us until it's verified."

"Did Sam have any more luck with the eagle drive?"

She sat down next to Rafe. "He hadn't when I left."

"That's a nice way of saying it." Rafe glared at Patrick.

Claire quickly changed the subject. "I tried to get to you in the hotel, but there was a stampede to the door and I lost you." She tucked a lock of hair behind her ear. "When I saw you unconscious I was so scared you wouldn't live through this."

Rafe picked up her hand and twined their fingers together. "Thoughts of Luke?"

Tears rose in Claire's throat. She nodded. "I'm glad you're alive." He squeezed her hand and the last few days of worry caught up with her. A tear escaped and rolled down her cheek. He turned toward her, his shoulders partially shielding her from the view of anyone else in the room. He lightly brushed the tear away with his thumb, his expression sympathetic. It was almost too much. She'd been through too much. Claire closed her eyes, trying to get control of her emotions so she didn't crumple into his arms and sob like a baby. "Ludin has been having secret meetings with my father."

"What?" He wrinkled his brow, obviously a bit surprised at the change in subject.

"After you were taken, he insisted on talking to my dad alone, then they've been having whispered arguments every time they're in a room together. I couldn't hear what was going on, though."

"Do you think he's involved with Bez?"

She had to give him credit—he didn't push her to share her thoughts or emotions and followed her lead. *At least in conversation.* "I don't know what to think at this point." She shifted closer to him as rocks started to pour in from the hole in the ceiling. A rope appeared, anchored by the guard as Bez climbed down.

He jumped to the ground and surveyed the room. "Isn't this a cozy little group?" He pulled a large black bag from off his shoulder. "Just so you are aware, we are not alone." He pointed up at the guard. "He has a gun and it would be like shooting fish in a barrel so don't try anything." He unzipped the bag and turned to a shaking and sweaty Patrick. "How are you feeling?"

Patrick scowled. "What do you care?"

Bez approached him. "Because I need some information from you. Then I'll give you what you so obviously need." He took out a syringe. "Do you want it?"

Patrick stared at it, licking his lips, his hand involuntarily reaching out. "I wish I didn't. You don't know how bad I wish I didn't need it."

Bez laughed. "If you tell me what I want to know, I'll give it to you."

With a wary look, he stood to face Bez. "I don't know anything else. I've done everything you've asked me to do. Just let us go."

Bez turned and pulled out the same sort of bomb vest Claire had seen strapped to Gary on that roof. "The information you gave us before wasn't complete. I want to be able to replicate the Black Widow specifications exactly and with the experiments setting them off in Connecticut, we aren't there yet. I know you've seen the plans." He pushed it toward Patrick, but he instinctively backed up.

Julie Coulter Bellon

"You mean killing Gary and blowing up my house and the office was an experiment?" Rafe didn't even sound surprised anymore, just resigned. Bez didn't bother to answer him.

"I can't work on a live bomb. I'm an informations analyst," Patrick pointed out.

"Oh, I'm not asking you to work on a live bomb. This is just to motivate you." He held up the remote. "My insurance policy. If you supply me with the information I will let you live. If not, this vest will make your death painless. Put it on."

"How am I supposed to tell you what I don't know?"

Bez pulled out a small roll of papers from his pants pocket that looked like they had plan specs on them. "Just fill in the blanks. That's all."

"No. I won't do it." Patrick moaned as Bez held out the syringe. His whole body seemed to shake at the mere sight of the heroin. "Please."

With a flick of his finger, the bomb activated. "You see, I control your life now. When I put this vest on you, there will be sixty seconds to make up your mind. Enough time for me to get out safely, of course. And there won't be any of your silly rhymes of warning like I gave Mr. Holman." He started to walk to the rope. "Be ready to pull me up," he called up to the guard.

Claire scrambled to her feet. "He's too sick to give you what you want, Bez. He'll tell you anything just to get the heroin."

"Then what use are any of you?" He took two steps toward Claire, his face angry.

Claire took a step back. "I'm the daughter of the NCS chief. I make a good bargaining chip."

She heard Rafe's intake of breath behind her, but she didn't look at him. Her entire focus was on Bez.

"Yes, I know exactly who you are. That's why I had you brought here. But I am surprised you would offer to stay as my hostage." Bez clicked on the remote and the bomb powered down.

In that moment, Claire understood what her brother had been thinking when he stared death in the face, a hostage himself, and oddly, she felt completely peaceful with what she was about to do. "If you let everyone else go, then yes, I will stay as your hostage."

Bez held up the vest. "Prove it to me."

Rafe tried to get to his feet, but Bez shoved him down. Claire heard him gasp in pain and knew what she had to do.

"No, Claire. Not like this." Rafe's voice was worried, urgent.

Claire hesitated for a brief second. "You'll let everyone else go?"

"You have my word." Bez put the vest on her shoulders, the weight of it heavier than she thought.

"Don't believe him, Claire. He's lying." When she finally looked back at him, he was holding one of his arms with the other, his face showing the agony he was feeling.

"It's okay, Rafe. I've got this."

Bez clicked the vest closed and held the remote to her face. "Maybe we can finish what we started on the roof. If I remember correctly, our conversation was cut short."

The image of Gary's last moments on the roof came to her mind, but she pushed those away. This was different. It was her sacrifice. And now it was between her and Bez.

Chapter Twenty

Rafe felt his flesh crawl as he watched Bez put the vest on Claire. *What is she thinking?* "I'm not leaving, no matter what you say."

"You'll do as you're told," Bez said, never taking his eyes off Claire. He reached out and touched Claire's cheek. Every muscle in Rafe's body bunched in anger. He moved to stand, wanting to get between Claire and Bez, but before he'd even gotten his feet under him, Patrick tackled Bez, knocking him to the ground.

"Leave her alone!" He threw punches wildly, as Bez screamed for his guard. "I'm not going to let you kill her like you killed Gary."

Vince started toward them. "Stay back, Vince," Rafe commanded.

"Shoot him!" Bez howled as he tried to fend off Patrick's blows.

"Patrick, look out!" Claire yelled as she stood near the men who were now rolling on the ground. When Patrick was on top, she bent to try and pry him off Bez. They all jumped as the gunshots echoed through the cave.

Rafe's heart was beating so hard he could barely catch a breath. He scrambled to Claire's side. "Are you okay?" She nodded and he crushed her to him, the vest bulky between them. He couldn't lose her now. Not here in this cave. "What were you thinking?" he said into her hair.

Patrick was nearly hysterical, trying to stop the blood trickling from the bullet wound in his calf. "I'm shot, I'm shot," he moaned. "Please, I need something to help me with the pain."

Bez got up, wiping the blood from his nose. He stood in the middle of the room, glaring at them. "The next person to try something like that will die." He held up the remote. "Or you'll all watch Claire die." Walking over to Patrick, he pulled out the papers. "Give me what I want. Now."

Patrick was crying openly now. "Give me the heroin first. You shot me."

"You deserved it." He threw the papers at Patrick's feet and crouched down with a pen in his hand, waving it under Patrick's nose. "I need those plans. Chapa will spot any imitation. I want the real thing. The power of the American Black Widow."

Don't do it, Rafe thought. But Patrick was a quivering mass and Rafe knew he wouldn't be able to resist. Just as he thought, Patrick took the pen from Bez's hand.

"Okay, I'll do it."

Rafe shook his head. "When Patrick gives you the information, you need to take the vest off of Claire."

"Shut up." Bez stood over Patrick, like a gratified conqueror looking over his war spoils.

"Sir, your guest is here," the guard called down to Bez.

"Excellent. And we have news for him."

Who would he invite here? Rafe's curiosity was piqued. *Would Chapa risk it?*

I have what you want," a male voice called out from above. "Do I have to come down?"

"Yes, come down," Bez invited. "I have news for you."

Rafe heard the man grunt as he descended the rope with lightning speed. He couldn't see the man's face, but he recognized that voice. "I knew it." The newcomer turned to face them, the scowl still on his face from the last time Rafe had seen him. "You were in on this all along, Ludin."

Ludin ignored him and walked toward Bez. "What a mess you've made of everything. Too many complications," he said, motioning to the people in the room. He reached into his pocket and brought out the eagle flash drive. "I told you I'd deliver."

"Don't," Rafe said, his mouth as dry as the dirt under his feet. Bez had everything he needed. The flash drive. And Ludin's knowledge that all it required for decryption was Vince's fingerprint. Bez would have the list of everyone he needed for another attack on the U.S. Rafe reached out for the drive, but Bez snatched it out of Ludin's hands.

"How do you know this is the right one and not the one that was already given to me?"

"Please. I've been working with them since they set foot in this country." He pointed to the drive. "With your leadership and the names on that list, maybe the U.S. will have a reason to leave our country. Fear is a powerful weapon and once we make the initial attack, we'll have the Americans waiting for the other shoe to drop." Ludin's eyes were cold as he looked at Rafe. "Let the girl go so she can be a messenger as to what happened here. We'll kill the rest."

Bez looked around at Rafe, Vince, and Patrick. "Excellent thoughts, but the girl is still useful to me."

"You promised you'd let everyone else go if put on the vest," Claire said as she stood and approached Bez. "You gave me your word."

"I lied." Bez took hold of the rope. "I have to verify the encryption key, but don't worry, I'll be back for you." He held up the remote. "And if anyone gets any ideas, the bomb will go off and there won't even be pieces of you left for anyone to find."

Claire grabbed for the remote, but he pushed her to the ground. She fell to her knees in front of the rope. Rafe reached for her, but Bez kicked his hand away. "Don't try me. I'm the angel of death, remember?"

Ludin stood next to her, and he reached down to help her up. When she was standing, he motioned her toward Rafe. With the rope in hand, it looked as if he were going to go up first. Giving it some slack, he then jerked the rope so hard the unsuspecting guard fell into the pit, hitting the ground with a loud thwack. The gun skittered out of his hand, near where Rafe was sitting and he lunged for it. The guard kicked out, grazing Rafe's shoulder. Rafe immediately felt a numbing sensation in his hand as he met his pain threshold and flew past it, the sensation of nails being ground into his shoulder blade hitting him full force. He tried to grab the gun, but it was like his hand couldn't follow his direction anymore.

Ludin threw one end of the rope around Bez's neck and quickly pressed a knife to his carotid artery. Bez was as still as a statue, looking as surprised as Claire felt. "What are you doing, Ludin?"

"Something I've wanted to for a long time," Ludin growled, bringing Bez closer.

The small, but obviously sharp knife pierced his neck, making a little drop of blood appear. "You're going to die for your crimes."

The guard raised the gun. "Let him go."

"We're partners. We're about to get everything we've ever wanted. Chapa will see our power, he'll pay for the bombs and the drugs and we'll have enough to carry out the amir's wishes. Our dreams will come true." Bez's voice was high, almost shrill.

"Your death is my dream."

The vest Claire was wearing suddenly powered up. "I won't die alone," Bez said. "Unless you let me go, the bomb will go off and bury this cave."

The guard adjusted his aim and Ludin made sure Bez was in front of him. "Give me the remote."

"Shoot him!" Bez commanded his guard. "Take the shot!"

"I wouldn't trust him," Ludin said in Bez's ear, turning slightly away from the guard. "He shot the last guy in the leg."

Rafe reached for Claire, looking over the vest. It was almost the same as Gary's, but there was something different in the triggering device. He rubbed his fingertips together. "I think I can get this off," he whispered.

Vince appeared behind him. "Can I help?" He glanced over at Ludin and Bez. "We have to do something."

"Thirty seconds, Ludin. I don't care if I die along with you and the Americans. At least the amir's file will be safe from anyone's prying eyes and our cells in America will live on to fight."

He pointed the knife at the guard. "Are you going to take the shot?"

The guard looked at Bez, then angled his aim and pulled the trigger.

Rafe tried to cover Claire, pulling her closer to him. He felt her put an arm around him, trying to cocoon him in her embrace, just as he had on that roof. *Stubborn woman!* It was so clear in that moment that if these were his last breaths on earth, he wanted to spend them with Vince and Claire.

The guard's shots were deafening, and someone was screaming. Rafe quickly realized that someone was shooting down the hole as well. Bullets seemed to be whizzing by them, the ricochets going wild. Rafe kept his hand on Claire's head, praying no bullets would hit them. He heard someone yell, "Stop shooting!" as if they were reading his thoughts. Claire pressed closer to him and he could feel the buzz of the vest powering down against his chest. Finally something was going right.

And then it was silent.

"Claire, are you all right?" Her father's voice rang out from above them, strong and clear. Rafe had never been so glad to hear another person's voice.

"I'm right here, Dad." She called back. Her father's head appeared in the hole.

"Thank you," he breathed as he closed his eyes.

She pulled back from her embrace with Rafe, looking into his face. "Are you okay?"

He spoke at the same time. "Are you hit?"

"I guess we're both fine then," she said with a smile.

"Vince?" Rafe said, trying to twist around and see his brother. "Are you okay?"

Vince looked down at his bleeding arm. "I'm hit, but I think I'm okay."

Rafe turned around so quick it made him a little dizzy. He examined his little brother's wound. Through and through. "That was too close."

"I just want to get out of here," Vince said grimly. "And never come back."

"That makes two of us." Rafe glanced over to where Ludin and the guard had been in the standoff. From his vantage point, it was easy to see the gaping bullet hole in Bez. He was dead. His guard wasn't moving either. "Looks like Ludin was on our side after all."

Claire, who had been hovering between Vince and Rafe, followed his gaze. Ludin was on the ground near Bez. "Hey, I think his chest is still moving. Ludin?" She disengaged from Rafe and went to his side.

Ludin grabbed her hand and pulled her closer. "I had to avenge my sister," he gasped out. "I suspected Patrick was the weak link and wanted to use him as bait. Your father said no. And then you were kidnapped. He listened to me after that." Claire had to bend to hear him, his voice fading. "My sister was addicted to the heroin and she died of an overdose. I failed her."

"You didn't fail her," Claire soothed.

"Is Bez dead?" Ludin twisted his head around to try and see Bez, but could only curl up and cough. "I didn't think that idiot guard would fire. Really, I didn't. Then everyone started shooting." He turned away from Claire. "I needed to stall until your father could follow my tracker. Bez should have stood trial for his crimes."

"Shh, don't talk now," Claire advised. She took the knife out of his hands, putting it on the ground. She picked up something small from the floor where she'd put the knife and let out a small gasp.

"What is that?" Rafe asked, watching her.

She held up the remote. Or what was left of it, all shot up. "I wondered why the bomb powered down all of the sudden. I don't think we can fix it." She looked down at her vest. "If there's a secondary trigger, though, we're going to have to be careful." She looked over at Patrick who was still hunched over against the wall. "Patrick? Could you give me a hand here? We need to get Ludin out."

Patrick didn't respond. He didn't even move. Rafe's stomach sank.

"Patrick?" Rafe scooted over to him, doing his best not to make the pain in his knee any worse. He knew what he was going to find, but he hoped he was wrong. Rafe touched his shoulder and he fell back, a bullet wound plain to see on his forehead.

"Patrick," he said sadly. He wished it hadn't ended this way.

Claire came over to stand behind him. "Are you okay?"

"Vince is alive. We're alive. That's all that matters to me right now," he said, looking up at her. "Let's get out of here."

Her dad's face appeared at the opening again. "We've got ropes. Who's coming up first?"

"Ludin first, then Claire," Rafe said firmly. "She's wired to some explosives that we need to get off of her right away."

"Rafe is next, he's hurt badly and needs medical attention." Claire folded her arms. "I'm fine to wait a little longer."

"Don't argue with me," Rafe said.

"I'm not arguing, I'm telling you how this is going to go." She lifted Ludin under the shoulders and dragged him toward the opening. "Okay, Dad, send the ropes down."

"Do you need someone to come help you harness him?" her dad asked.

Claire caught the rope and harness. "No, I've got this."

Vince stood and did the best he could to help her. Rafe felt like he should be the one up and helping her, but he knew his mind wanted to do things his body couldn't. Even with the bulky vest, Claire was efficient and got Ludin ready to go. Before he knew it, the harness was coming back down for the next person.

"Rafe," she said, motioning him forward.

"Vince first," he countered. "Then you."

Rafe stood, leaning on Claire for support as they got Vince ready to be pulled out. "Thanks for not giving up on me," Vince said as he pulled on the rope to signal he was ready.

"I always have your back, little brother," Rafe said.

When Vince was almost out, Rafe tipped Claire's face up. "Please go next."

Claire took the eagle drive out of her pocket. "I think you need to get this back to my dad as soon as possible and get your knee looked at. I want you to be able to walk again. Please."

Rafe cupped her head with his hands and gently kissed her. "I'm only agreeing because you said please."

She smiled, letting her fingers rub over the stubble on his jawline. "I'll have to remember that little detail more often then." Claire bent down and handed Rafe Ludin's knife. "For safekeeping."

He folded down the sharp end and put it in his pocket with the eagle drive. When he was in the harness, he took one more look at her. "See you topside."

"I won't be long," she said.

Rafe was pulled toward the light, but he wouldn't feel relieved until Claire was there with him. He looked back when he was halfway there and was stunned to see the guard rising from the corner. "Claire, look out!"

Claire whirled, but it seemed like everything was happening in slow motion. They were grappling, but Claire couldn't defend herself well with that vest on. "Let me down," Rafe shouted, but the men pulling him either didn't hear or wouldn't listen. Rafe's attention was torn back to Claire when he heard an alarming yelp that was quickly cut short. The guard had her in a headlock and was choking her. "Let me down!" Rafe yelled.

"He's hurt. Bring him up quick so we can get someone else down there," he heard one voice say.

No way. Rafe pulled at the ropes, but he couldn't get out of the harness in mid-air. In a flash, he pulled out Ludin's knife and began sawing at it. *Please don't let me be too late.* He tried to meet Claire's eyes and hoped she could see what he was about to do. *Maybe I should try to warn her.* He hummed a quick verse of *Ring Around the Rosy* as he cut the rope. *Hang on!*

When the final thread snapped under the blade, Rafe tried to position himself right over the guard and he put his knee down. He fell hard, right on top of him. The man's neck snapped under the force of impact, and Rafe's knee felt like it snapped right along with it, but Rafe had the knife ready just in case. He crouched as best he could with one good knee, ready to defend Claire and himself, but the man was dead.

Rafe could hear Claire choking and gasping as she staggered toward him. "Claire?" He reached for her, but even that small movement sent a jolt of pain through him. Whatever parts of his body didn't hurt before, definitely hurt now. He knew he couldn't walk, but he could stand there and hold her. Barely. She stepped into his arms, her eyes watering and red, the guard's handprints still stark against the white of her neck.

Skip and two other men appeared at the opening. "What happened?"

Rafe was about to tell them everything was fine, now, and curse them for not listening earlier, when Claire's vest suddenly powered on. "No way," he breathed, glancing up at Claire's face. She looked as shocked as he felt. "We need to disarm this bomb, now, Skip. Do you have anyone up there familiar with munitions?"

"The bomb? On Claire?" For a moment he sounded like a frantic father, but he recovered quickly. "How much time do we have?" Skip asked, his tone neutral and professional.

Rafe looked at the timer. "About a minute. Maybe less." Even as Rafe said it, Claire didn't flinch. *She always surprises me.*

"I'll see what I can do. I'm coming down."

"No, Dad, don't. I've got this." She pulled the remote out of her pants pocket. "The remote was shot, but maybe it will still work," Claire said to Rafe, her voice barely more than a croak, but steady. She pressed on the button several times. Nothing happened.

Rafe moved her hands as he looked at the trigger. "If we can disable the trigger, we can get it off."

Claire looked down. "Give me the knife."

"What for?"

"Please don't question me right now."

Rafe handed her the knife and she quickly pried off the cover on the front panel. She was talking to herself. "Red, then blue. Or is it white first?"

"Is this from the seminar you took?"

202

She bent her head in concentration. "Hold this steady for me."

Rafe did as she asked, watching her work. He held the wires out and she fingered three of them, obviously trying to make a decision. "I'm going to cut the red, then the blue, then the white. Ready?"

Rafe quickly kissed her forehead. "Ready."

Claire started cutting. Rafe held her shoulders and closed his eyes. Even his lungs felt tight. He went completely still, holding his breath, not wanting to distract her. "Tell me when it's the last one." He opened his eyes.

She stared back at him. "Last one." With a flick of her wrist, she cut it. They both let out an audible sigh when the vest powered down. As soon as they were sure the trigger was disabled, Rafe immediately took the knife from her shaking hand and cut the Velcro straps. She helped him lift the vest off of her and set it on the floor. When she straightened, she rubbed her shoulders. Rafe took over, gently turning her to knead the tender skin where the vest had rested.

Claire's body leaned into his, but it was obvious he couldn't hold their weight. "We need to sit down."

Rafe agreed and sank down with her. "For a minute there, I didn't think we were going to make it," he murmured. He let his fingers comb through her hair. "Good thing you paid attention in that seminar."

She chuckled hoarsely. "I think I'm going to send my instructor a thank you note."

"I think he deserves flowers." Rafe leaned forward as men were scrambling above them, dirt and rocks spilling through the opening when several ropes came down. "Looks like the cavalry's here for us. Finally."

Claire turned in his arms. "Thanks for coming back for me." She looked toward the ceiling, then laughed before she ended in a coughing fit. "You really fell for me."

Rafe patted her back. "You're such a comedian."

She gave him a sympathetic look. "I know that must have cost you. You're in so much pain already. I'm sorry about your knee." She pressed her side closer to his chest as if she were suddenly exhausted and needed to lean on him. It felt good, especially when he thought about how close he came to losing her.

"I've never been so scared in my life. I was afraid I'd fall on *you*."

"I heard you humming that rhyme." She pressed her lips together. "I never want to hear '*Ring Around the Rosy*' again."

"Me neither." She tipped her face up to his and he raised his hand to cup her cheek. Holding her gaze, he gently pulled her toward him. She angled forward the last few inches, quickly closing the distance between them. She slid her arms around his neck and his lips moved over hers. The white-hot pain in his body faded away, quenched in Claire's arms. He pressed her closer. One thing was sure—he needed her in his life. Stubbornness and all.

"Claire, is everything all right?" Skip said as he made his way down the rope.

She barely pulled back, her forehead touching Rafe's, as if she felt the connection, too, and didn't want to break it, even with an audience. "Everything's fine, Dad. I told you, I've got this." And then she kissed Rafe again.

Epilogue

Rafe maneuvered his crutches through the doorway, heading for the serving area. He wasn't going to sit on the couch while Claire did all the work. He was sick of sitting.

"Hey, aren't you supposed to be elevating that leg and resting your shoulder?" Claire said as she came around the corner, giving him a quick kiss on the lips.

"I can't sit anymore," he told her. "I'm helping."

She brushed by him, but turned to wait. "Why don't you go sit at the table and pour some sparkling water into the glasses then?"

"That's still sitting," he grumbled.

Claire laughed. "I'm just helping you follow doctor's orders."

Rafe knew he was beaten, so he made his way to the table. "I shouldn't have told you what he said." He sat down, looking at the banner that covered the top half of one wall of the Veterans Community Center, 'Happy Retirement' in large red, white, and blue lettering. "Is retirement really happy, you think?" he said aloud.

"It depends on the person I imagine," Claire said as she put out more glasses. "I think my dad will love it. You, I'm not so sure about. That's why we're having a double retirement party for the two of you—sort of sending you into it on a positive note."

Rafe grimaced. "I keep trying to decide what I should do. The military has been my life for so long."

Colby, Bart, and Captain Reed came through the door, and Claire met them before they'd taken three steps in. "I'm so glad you could come." She gave them each a hug. "As much as it pains me to say it, I missed you guys. I could have used some backup."

"Which you would have gotten had you asked," Colby said, holding onto her a second longer. Rafe could see the relief in his face at Claire being home safe. He knew that look because he'd seen it in the mirror every day these last two weeks since they'd come home from Afghanistan. "How are you holding up? Colby asked.

"I'm fine. Rafe has a bit of recuperating to do." She drew them over to the table he was sitting at. "He's pouring drinks for us tonight so he can take it easy."

Rafe shook his head. "I won't be pouring drinks all night. The doctor said not to let the knee stiffen up. That means I'm going to have to move around at some point."

"You're lucky you're in one piece from what I hear," the captain said, picking up an hors d'oeuvre from the table.

"Yeah, well, I have to take an early retirement. My knee won't ever be what it used to be and you definitely need a knee in combat situations."

"But you will get full use of it," Claire cut in. "Good enough for a civilian life."

Vince came up from behind the group. "Is he still complaining about his knee?"

"I'm not complaining, the captain asked," Rafe countered. "Where's Penny tonight?"

Vince smiled. "She's on her way. Had a wardrobe malfunction to fix."

"High maintenance, man, I'm telling you right now." Rafe looked up at his little brother, grateful his bruises were fading, that he hadn't been hurt worse and that they had a second chance together. "Have you heard from Mom and Dad? I thought the government would never be done debriefing you."

"All I really needed to do was give them my fingerprint. With everything that was on that drive, Homeland Security, the CIA, the DoD, and whomever else will be busy for months rounding all those people up." He patted Rafe's good shoulder. "And you know more about Mom and Dad than I do. They were both surprised at how much you've been hovering over them. You've changed, man."

"I'm not hovering," Rafe grumbled. But Vince was right about one thing. He was different now. He'd been given a second chance at life and he was going to take it. He didn't want to have any regrets in his life or relationships. He looked over at Claire who was talking and laughing with Bart. Rafe didn't know what he had with Claire yet, but he knew he didn't want to wait to find out.

"What are you thinking about?" Claire asked as she came over to stand next to him.

"Just how much Afghanistan changed my outlook on life." He reached up to grab her hand and brought it to his lips. "For the better I think."

"Me, too," she said, her smile disappearing. "I got a lot of perspective on my brother's death. And on my own life."

Rafe moved his crutches to the side and stood up, bringing her into his embrace. They stood there, sharing the moment of understanding. They'd experienced something in Afghanistan that had bonded them together, but even before that, Rafe had known she was special. "I think we need to talk," he murmured against her ear.

"I think you talk too much." She put her hands on either side of his face and pulled him into a kiss.

He groaned good-naturedly as he heard laughter and clapping around them. *This is what I call living in the moment.* They broke apart, smiling, but not sorry. "I'll keep that in mind for future reference," he told her as he sat down again.

Skip came through the door with Marlene and Will, heading straight over to join them at the table. "It looks like this is where the party is. Thanks so much for doing this for me, Claire."

Claire hugged her dad and Rafe was sort of glad Skip had missed the kiss Claire had given him a moment before. He still felt like he needed to make up for punching him in the stomach when they first met.

"I know retirement will be a transition for you, Dad, but I think you did the right thing," Claire said, sitting down at the table next to Rafe.

"Well, I didn't have much choice. After the president found out what we'd done, he was pretty upset. Chain of command and all that. But, you're right, I think I did the right thing. I need to be with my family." He squeezed Will's shoulder. "We've got a lot of catching up to do."

Will gazed up at his dad, obviously happy, but he quickly disengaged himself when he saw a waitress carrying several dishes. "I'll go get us a plate of food."

"Don't eat it all before you bring it out," Claire called to his retreating back.

Rafe chuckled. "Good luck with that. He's a growing teenager."

Skip sat down in the chair next to Claire and Marlene sat on the other side of him. "So, have you decided what you're going to do with your retirement?" Skip asked.

Rafe slipped his arm around the back of Claire's chair. "First of all, I'm going to take Claire and Will to a hockey game and introduce them to the team. After that, we'll see. I'm sort of thinking I might ask Captain Reed if there are any consulting jobs I can do for his team. I've got some experience."

Claire looked over at him with a twinkle in her eye. "That's a horrible idea. Then I'd have to concentrate on saving your life all the time."

Rafe laughed. "I think I saved *your* life at least twice before you saved mine."

"No way," she said, shaking her head. "When?"

"I saved you on the roof and at the hotel bombing."

"I was doing just fine. I saved *you* on the roof if I recall correctly."

Skip leaned between them, using his hand to make a cutting motion. "Hey now, how about we call it a draw? You both saved each other."

Rafe looked at Claire, her beautiful brown hair down around her shoulders, her face smiling at him with such promise. "Deal."

"Deal," she agreed.

He touched her hair, motioning for her to come closer. Suddenly it didn't matter if her father was there. He kissed her, anyway, but made it a quick one.

Rafe left his arm around her, and when he glanced at Skip, Rafe was glad to see he didn't look like he minded. Maybe he wasn't holding a grudge after all. "So, did you wrap everything up today?"

Skip nodded. "Ludin is going to be fine. Last I heard they're probably going to make him some sort of director over unraveling the drug trade in Afghanistan. He'll still be working with the U.S. since it's becoming a problem with our soldiers." He looked down. "Patrick's body was released to his parents. They were pretty heartbroken."

Rafe clenched his jaw. It was still hard for him to believe how Patrick's choices had devastated so many people, but he did feel bad for his family. "I'm sorry to hear that. You know, as I was thinking about things, it had to have been Patrick that warned us right before the hotel bombing. He's the only other person that would have known the Ring Around the Rosy rhyme and what it meant to our unit. So, maybe in a way he was trying to redeem himself."

"I never want to hear that rhyme again," Vince said as he joined them.

Claire nodded. "I said that, too."

Vince held a package in his hand. "Rafe, I have something for you." He handed him the flat box.

"What is it?"

"Open it and find out."

Rafe carefully opened the box and pulled out a beautiful cherry wood plaque with Gary's picture on it with 'Friend and Hero' printed underneath it.

"He was a hero," Vince said softly. "And gave his life for his country and his friends. I thought we could honor him by hanging this in Axis offices when we reopen."

Rafe could hardly speak. Looking at his friend's face in the picture, smiling up at him, he knew Gary was at peace. And he was, too. "Thank you, Vince." The lump in his throat grew larger. "If I can't get a job anywhere else, can I still come work with you? Maybe I can run security or something." His voice was gravelly, but Rafe was proud he'd contained his emotion.

"Look in the bottom of the box," Vince said, pointing.

Rafe pulled out a tie and everyone at the table laughed.

"Of course you can come work at Axis if you'll commit to certain wardrobe changes," Vince teased.

When the laughter stopped, Vince got serious. "We'd be glad to have you. I hope you know that." He glanced at the door then got up from the table. "Penny's here, I'll see you later."

Rafe shook his head, watching the two of them. Penny was dressed the same way she'd been when he'd met her at the office. She stroked her brother's arm and gave him a kiss in greeting. Who knew? Maybe they would work out. He was thinking positive.

Skip got up to talk to more guests and pretty soon Rafe and Claire were alone at the table. He took her hand. "Do you think anyone would notice if we left early?"

"Why, does your knee hurt? Do you need to go home?"

He turned her hand over and caressed her palm with his thumb. "No, there's a midnight showing of the *Princess Bride* tonight."

Claire bit her lip. "You don't know how tempting that is. I love that movie."

"Just say yes. Or as you wish." He grinned. "I seem to remember you saying you didn't think I was the type of guy who could relax and enjoy that movie. Now's my chance to prove you wrong." He leaned in, his voice low and persuasive. "Come on, it will be fun. Then we can quote it for the rest of the week."

Before Claire could reply, Bart, Colby, and the captain came toward them. She pulled her hand back and stood up. "Uh oh," she murmured.

"We've got a call," the captain said. "Situation about three blocks over. Two hostages." He drew his brows together. "Sorry to take you away from the party. I can try and call in someone else. Maybe Steve?"

"No, it's fine, my dad will understand." Claire turned back to Rafe. "Rain check?"

The captain stepped toward Rafe and leaned over a bit. "You can ride along if you like."

"Sir?" Rafe and Claire both said together.

"Strictly observing, of course," the captain clarified.

"You in?" Claire asked Rafe. She raised her eyebrows and gave him a questioning look.

"All in," Rafe stood up and put a little weight on his knee before he grabbed his crutches. It felt better. *He* felt better. And he knew a lot of that had to do with Claire and the future he hoped to have with her.

"We'll be right there." She reached for her purse and pulled out an elastic band. Before Rafe could blink she had her hair in a messy ponytail. He tucked a stray lock behind her ear, unable to keep the smile off his face. He had fallen and come home. For good.

ABOUT THE AUTHOR

Julie Coulter Bellon loves to write international romantic suspense novels because she gets to travel to distant lands to research and add an authentic feel to all of her books. Her favorite cities so far are Athens, Paris, Ottawa, and London. She taught journalism at BYU for fourteen years and that kept her on the cutting edge of current events and world news—which is where she gets her story ideas.

Julie offers writing and publishing tips, as well as her take on life on her blog http://ldswritermom.blogspot.com You can also find out about all her upcoming projects at her website www.juliebellon.com or you can follow her on Twitter @juliebellon

Made in the USA
Charleston, SC
19 November 2012